Charming the Widow

LOVE IN APPLE BLOSSOM
BOOK THREE

KIT MORGAN

Charming the Widow

(Love in Apple Blossom, Book 3)

© 2022 Kit Morgan

Cover design by Angel Creek Press and EDH Designs

❀ Created with Vellum

License Note

Chapter One

The widow Crawford's farm, Apple Blossom, Montana Territory, 1879

Sarah Crawford brushed a lock of blonde hair out of her eyes and continued with the washing. Too bad she didn't live in the middle of town – she could take in more laundry. But being over a quarter mile outside of Apple Blossom wasn't so bad. She took Caleb's old wheelbarrow and the children to town every other day to gather laundry, tidy up the saloon for the captain if he needed it, let the children have their lessons, then return home and start the washing and mending. It didn't bring in much, but it was all she could do.

She wiped the sweat from her brow with the back of her hand and continued scrubbing. She was washing Mr.

Featherstone's clothes today and would deliver them to him tomorrow. Mrs. Featherstone would have another load ready for her, no doubt, as would the captain. She should take advantage while the Darlings were in town and offer her laundry and mending services. It would bring in a little extra income, and everyone knew she could use the money.

She stopped scrubbing, looked around the backyard, and hoped Flint or Lacey would answer the door if one of the Darling men showed up today. One of them was still working on Sheriff Cassie Laine's house, and from what she'd heard, it was coming along nicely. Dora Jones at the hotel told her she should have a look the next time she was in town, and she planned to. But she didn't like having to speak with strangers – she became nervous around them. The Englishmen currently residing in Apple Blossom were polite enough, but she still didn't trust them.

In fact, she didn't really trust anyone.

She thought of Caleb, his funeral, the months of heavy sorrow that followed. She and Caleb might not have had the best marriage, but they got along well enough. They both wanted children, and together they could survive. Now that she was alone, she wasn't so sure.

She hung Mr. Featherstone's pants on the clothes-line, returned to the washtub and picked up another pair of trousers. She often wondered if she'd spend the rest of her life washing, ironing, and doing mending for others.

If so, she'd just have to be satisfied with it. The work put food on the table and kept a roof over their heads.

She looked at the house. Where were Flint and Lacey? She left her wash station – a washtub atop an old table – and headed for the back porch. She wanted to make sure Mr. Darling was let in. She had so many things that needed fixing and wasn't sure where to have him start.

Truth was, she didn't want him to begin at all, too nervous to have a strange man in her home. But Captain Stanley assured her he'd personally check on the man's progress and make sure Mr. Darling was doing his best for her. "Thank the Lord for Captain Stanley," she said as she headed into the kitchen.

Flint and Lacey were at the table eating cookies and drinking milk. "Hello, Mama," Lacey greeted her. "Are you done working? Can we go to the creek now?"

"No, sweetheart." She went to the table and took a cookie from the jar. "I'm waiting for Mr. Darling to show up, remember?"

Flint's eyes went wide. "That's today?"

"It is." She looked suspiciously at her son. "Why are you so surprised?"

He shook his head. "No reason. Do I get to help him?"

"That remains to be seen. After all, how much help can you be?"

"Billy helped Mr. Conrad Darling," Flint said. "He even got paid!"

Sarah smiled at her son. "That's all well and good, Flint, but I don't know what *this* Mr. Darling is going to do yet. If you'd like to offer your services, then go right ahead. Just don't be disappointed if he tells you no." She took a bite of cookie and waited for Flint to digest that bit of advice.

He drained his milk. "All right. I'll ask. I hope I get paid."

Sarah took another bite of cookie, looked at it and made a face. It was stale. She'd have to make a new batch, which meant she'd have to get more flour from Alma Kirk's general store.

"Mama," Lacey said.

"Yes, sweetie?"

Lacey held up her doll, Mrs. Winkle. "Can we help?"

Sarah smiled. "You're so adorable, how can Mr. Darling refuse? However, I don't think Mrs. Winkle can swing a hammer."

Lacey looked at her doll and shook a finger at it. "You told me you could do anything. You said you could build a whole house."

Flint laughed. "No, she can't. For one, she's too short."

Sarah put her fist to her mouth to keep from laughing. Her children were her whole world and she'd do anything for them. She just prayed she could keep doing laundry and mending for the folks in Apple Blossom. Otherwise, she didn't know how they'd make it. She and

Caleb had put a little money away, but it was almost gone.

Before she could lament further, there was a knock at the door. "That must be him. Now, children, I want you to be on your best behavior. You promise?"

Flint and Lacey exchanged a look she hadn't seen before. If she didn't have to answer the door, she'd start questioning them. She hoped they weren't up to something. "Do you?" she prompted.

Flint nodded. "We promise."

Lacey held up her doll. "Even Mrs. Winkle promises."

"That's good to know." She cut through the combination parlor/dining room and answered the door. "Mr. Darling. How good of you to come."

He took off his hat. Even she had to admit that all the Darlings were handsome and well-mannered. Still, they were strangers as far she was concerned and shouldn't be trusted. The sooner he got his work done the better. "Good afternoon, Mrs. Crawford. I'm Irving Darling in case you've forgotten which of us you were getting."

"You make it sound as if I won you in a lottery." She motioned him to come inside and closed the door. This was the part she was dreading. "As you can see, the place isn't much." Indeed it wasn't. Though clean, the furniture was shabby, the sofa and chairs wobbly, and the curtains had become a nesting place for moths.

Mr. Darling took in the room. "How long have you lived here?"

Too long, came to mind, but she wasn't going to voice that. "Ever since Caleb and I married. He lived here before I arrived. His family built the place years ago."

His eyebrows shot up. "Arrived?"

She nodded and played with a loose thread on her apron. "I was a mail-order bride."

He nodded and continued his perusal of her shabby little home. "You have just the one room here."

"And a kitchen," she said as if he was daft. She took a calming breath. "That is, yes, as far as formal areas go. Then we have the kitchen and the two bedrooms."

"Four rooms." He looked at the entrance to the kitchen. There was no door, and one got a good view of the cookstove. "Where are the bedrooms?"

She went to a door at the other end of the parlor and opened it. "Lacey and Flint sleep here."

He joined her and peeked inside. "And your room?"

"Off the kitchen." She fiddled with the same thread again and finally pulled it.

He didn't say anything for a moment before he went to the front door.

She gasped. "You're leaving already?"

"No, I want to get another look at the porch. You've got a couple of steps that need repairing. Now I want to see what else I'll have to do."

"Oh, yes," she said, blushing. "Of course." She started to twist the thread she'd pulled. She wished she wasn't so nervous but couldn't help it. She followed him onto the porch and pointed at a couple of boards she knew needed replacing. "There's one there, another's here. If you have the time, I know there's some on the far side. Then there's the back porch."

He looked at the other end, nodded, then got back to studying the boards she'd showed him. "These look rotten. They'll have to be replaced."

"Caleb was going to get around to those, but then ..."

He smiled warmly. "I know." He went to the other end of the porch.

She watched him go, her heart in her throat. It wasn't that she was about to cry over Caleb. No, she was reacting to the unexpected kindness in his voice, the look of warmth in his eyes.

"Your railing isn't so good either."

She crossed the porch to him. "No, it has seen better days. In fact, the entire house is wretched. I know this and don't expect you to take on the whole thing. It would take weeks, months ..."

"Or a match," he teased.

She laughed nervously. "Yes, or that. Captain Stanley's made the same remark on several occasions. Unfortunately, this ramshackle little cabin is all I have."

"I understand," he said gently. "Rest assured, I'll do my best." He nodded and headed for the porch steps. "I'm going to fetch some tools. I'll be back shortly."

Sarah watched him go, heart pounding. Why was she so nervous? But deep down she knew why and would have to do her best to get through this.

Irving hopped on his horse Patch and headed for Letty's place. It was easier to go there and gather what he needed than return to town. Most of the tools they'd been using to fix up her barn and house were still on the premises.

The Widow Crawford's place would take a lot of work. A match, in truth, would be easier. But they didn't have time to build a new home for the woman, so he'd do what he could and leave it at that. From the looks of things, the roof leaked, some of the floorboards in the children's bedroom would have to be replaced, and Heaven only knew what shape the kitchen and the other bedroom were in, not to mention the back porch.

There was no getting around the fact that he'd need help. His brothers Conrad and Phileas were putting the finishing touches on Cassie's home. If he could tear Sterling away from Letty long enough, he'd get some help from him. Otherwise, he'd coerce Wallis and Oliver into helping.

His biggest concern was the children getting in his way. Conrad got smart and was able to utilize Billy Watson to help him. But the lad was a good worker and listened to instructions. He wasn't so sure about the widow's two children. For one, the boy was younger than Billy. What could a six-year-old do?

"What are you doing here?" Letty said as he rode into the barnyard. She left the front porch and headed for him. "Sterling is in the barn."

Irving tipped his hat. "Thanks, Letty." He dismounted, wrapped Patch's reins around the hitching post, then headed that way. "I just came to get a few tools. I'm starting work on the Widow Crawford's house today."

"I'm glad." She trotted after him. "Don't take it wrong if Sarah's a little standoffish."

Irving stopped and turned around. "She seemed nervous."

"It's just that she and Caleb, well, they had a different sort of relationship." She stuck her hands in her apron pockets and sighed. "She was a mail-order bride, and they didn't really get along at first."

"They must have done fine after a while," he said. "They have two children."

"That's true. They both wanted children. Just be kind, Irving, that's all I'm saying." She smiled. "I made coffee. Come up to the house and have some before you head back."

He smiled. "Thank you, I will." He continued to the barn and found Sterling cleaning out a stall. "Greetings, brother."

Sterling stopped and leaned against the pitchfork he was using. "Irving, what brings you here?"

"I need some tools." He started looking around. "For the Widow Crawford's house."

Sterling set the pitchfork against the stall wall. "Then you'll need nails, a hammer, a saw ... let's see, and a few other things." He went to a large box and began to rifle through it. "Oliver tossed a lot of stuff in here." He handed Irving a hammer.

"Thanks. Where did he put the nails?" Irving continued to look around.

"Over by the chopping block. We can put some in a sack." Sterling disappeared into another stall and emerged with a saw. "Need some lumber?"

"I need to take measurements first. But I will need some." Irving started a pile of tools and thought of what he could fit into his saddlebags. "If you don't need any of this over the next few days, then I'll leave everything at her house. It will be easier than coming here to fetch them every day."

"Sure, go ahead." Sterling walked to the barn's wide entrance, looked at the pasture beyond, and sighed. "I want to stay."

Irving almost dropped the can of nails. "What did you say?"

His brother turned around. "You know how much I love Letty. You also know we're going to marry before the rest of you leave."

"Rest of us, is it? So you've decided, then?" Dread settled in Irving's gut. He added the can to the other tools and fought his rising panic.

"I'm going to sleep on it a while longer, but yes. It's what I'd *like* to do." Sterling sighed again. "Irving, I know this isn't what you wanted to hear."

"You have no idea." He didn't mean to sound terse; it just came out that way. "I'm not ready for this."

"If it makes you feel any better, neither am I."

"Yes, but you're not the one who's going back to England to face Father and Mother, then be saddled with all that goes with it." Irving turned on his heel and went back to the pile of tools. He'd have to wrap the saw in something – it wouldn't fit in a saddlebag. The hammer he'd like to throw at Sterling but knew that wouldn't solve anything. Sterling's happiness meant his misery and that was that. "Maybe you should sleep on it a good solid week or more."

"I can help you," Sterling said.

Irving laughed and turned around. "In what, a week, maybe two if we stay longer? How are you going to teach me everything Father has taught you over half your lifetime?"

"You wouldn't be the only second son to have to take over an estate unprepared. And you're forgetting that Father is still very much alive. He has a lot of years left in him, Irving. Time to teach you plenty."

Irving took a deep breath and let it out slowly. "All right, there's that. But then I'll have to put up with Mother and you know how she is."

"Tell her you're not ready for marriage. That you want to spend your days learning how to run the estate to be the next Viscount Darlington."

Irving spied a small sack and began putting nails in it. "Have you told the others?"

"No." He leaned against a nearby post. "I'm going to wait."

"In case you change your mind?" Irving stuck his hand back into the can and pricked his finger. He shook his hand out then checked it for any signs of damage. If this was how the rest of his day was going to go, he should return to the hotel and go back to bed. No, it was too late in the day for that. Bother.

Sterling came away from the post. "I'm waiting so you'll have more time to adjust to the idea."

"How considerate of you," Irving shot back.

"Come now, brother. It's not that bad. I know how you like to have everything perfect before you take a project on. In fact, one of us should have warned Mrs. Crawford about you."

Irving narrowed his eyes. "Very funny."

"We all know how you can get – even you know." Sterling walked to the barn entrance again. "This place is peaceful, brother. Life is slower here. There's something about it that I can't explain ..." He turned to him. "It calls to me."

Irving gaped at him. "Smelly cows, sour milk, and a much-improved rickety house?"

Sterling smiled. "And Letty."

Okay, he had to concede that. "Very well, you're madly in love with her and everything else around here." He gathered the nails, hammer, saw and a few other things, then headed for Patch.

"Are you going to have a cup with us?" Sterling called after him.

Irving turned around. "Is there pie?"

Sterling smiled. "There is."

Irving made a show of rolling his eyes. "Then as the next Viscount Darlington, I shall deign to have a slice with you and your future bride." He started for his horse again. "But that doesn't mean I have to like any of this!"

"You'll learn to love it," Sterling said.

He dumped the tools near Patch. "Did you?"

Sterling crossed the barnyard to stand in front of him. "Yes, I did. Which is why I'm not taking this decision lightly."

So, he had to give him that too. Sterling wasn't one to make rash decisions. "The others will be upset."

"Are you?"

Irving shoved the hammer and sack of nails into one of the saddlebags. "Of course I am. You're asking me to take on a title and a huge estate because *you* want to get married. Have you considered taking Letty back to England?"

"Of course. But I don't know if she'll like it." Sterling gazed at the house. "She's such a part of this place."

"You could make her part of our place too," Irving argued. "For Heaven's sake, take her home, see if she likes it. Then you'll know."

"And if she doesn't?"

"Then we'll all know, won't we?" Irving stuffed the last of the tools into the saddlebags and headed back to the barn.

"Where are you going?" Sterling asked.

"To get a gunnysack for the saw." He kept walking

and hoped Sterling didn't follow. With any luck he'd go into the house.

By the time Irving returned to his horse, there was no sign of his brother. Good. He wrapped the saw, left it near the hitching post, then went to grab a cup of coffee. He knew Sterling wouldn't say a word while they were with Letty, which meant he didn't have to think about it. Maybe working on the Widow Crawford's house wouldn't be so bad after all. It would give him something to do and keep his mind off the inevitable: that like it or not, he was going to be the next Viscount Darlington.

Chapter Two

S arah finished Mr. Featherstone's laundry and had it drying on the clothesline when she re-entered the house. "Has Mr. Darling returned?"

"No, Mama," Lacey said. "And Mrs. Winkle is getting impatient."

Sarah folded her arms and smiled at her. "Does Mrs. Winkle have an appointment with Mr. Darling?"

"No, but he said he'd be right back." Lacey hugged her doll and ran from the kitchen.

Sarah followed. There was no sign of Flint, and she was beginning to wonder where he'd gotten to. She found him sitting on the front steps. "What are you doing out here?"

"I'm waiting for Mr. Darling to come back. Maybe I can hand him his tools or something."

Sarah took a deep breath. She wasn't sure she wanted Flint pestering the man. "I'm glad you want to help but be sure you ask him. If he tells you no, respect his answer."

"I will, Ma." He focused on the gate with an unwavering stare.

Sarah did her best not to laugh and returned to the kitchen. Before she started another batch of laundry, she needed a cup of coffee. She got a pot going on the stove and looked at what few stale cookies remained in the jar. "Hmm, do I have everything I need to make a new batch?" While she waited for the coffee to boil, she went into her small larder to see what ingredients she had. Not many.

With a sigh she went to her room, dug out her small jewelry box, and checked her money. If she skimped, she could make a pound of flour last a couple of weeks. But she had to have something to serve Mr. Darling while he worked. It was only right, as he was doing the work for free.

She made a list of what she needed, then went to the porch steps again. Flint hadn't moved a muscle. "Any sign of him?"

"Not yet. But when I see him, I'll come get you." He twisted around to look at her. "What's that?"

She waved the list in her hand. "Something that says I need to go to the general store."

He left the steps. "Are you going to make cookies?"

"Yes. For Mr. Darling. Which means you can't eat them all, is that understood?" She stuffed the list into her apron pocket.

"Aww ..." Flint groaned.

"Hello there!"

Sarah and Flint turned toward the gate as Mr. Darling came through it. He had saddlebags slung over one shoulder and was carrying a wrapped bundle. "I'm sorry it took so long," he said. "I decided to get the tools we left at Letty's place rather than go to the hotel and discover I'd have to go to Letty's anyway."

"That makes sense." She watched him approach. My, he was a handsome thing. She blushed and lowered her gaze

Flint smiled at him. "Ma says I can help!"

She gasped. "Flint Michael, I said no such thing. I told you to *ask* if you could help."

"Can I?" He looked brightly at Mr. Darling. "Please?"

Mr. Darling smiled. "You've been talking to Billy Watson, haven't you?"

Flint nodded vigorously and grinned.

Sarah covered her mouth for a moment. "I'm sorry." She dropped her hand. "It's just that Billy's been bragging about how much work he and your brother have done on Cassie's house. The other children view him now like a grown-up."

"I scc," Mr. Darling said. "But does Flint have any idea how hard Billy worked?"

She eyed Flint, then looked at Mr. Darling again. "Somehow I doubt Flint understands the extent of Billy's labors."

Mr. Darling slid the saddlebags off his shoulder and onto the porch with a loud *thunk*. "Let's see if I can recall everything Billy did. He had to scrape paint, carry furniture out to the backyard, wallpaper, paint of course, and he had to dust and clean and wash and scrub and ..."

"Hey," Flint blurted. "Billy never said he did all that."

Mr. Darling bent to him. "Well, lad, he did. He worked very hard which is why my brother Conrad paid him. Are you willing to work that hard?"

Flint's eyes darted to his mother and back. "If Billy can do it, so can I. So what if he's a year older?"

"You don't have to let him," Sarah said.

"I'll give the boy a chance." Mr. Darling set the bundle off to one side. "The first thing you can do, young man, is get a hammer out of my saddlebags."

"Yes, sir!" Flint hurried to comply.

Lacey came out of the house holding Mrs. Winkle. "Can we help?"

Sarah thought she'd better come to his rescue. Flint might be a handful; having both her children try to help would be too much. "I need your assistance in the kitchen, young lady." She gave Mr. Darling a knowing smile. "I have cookies to bake."

"Cookies!" Lacey chimed. "What kind?"

"Molasses, but we'll have to get a few things." She looked at the saddlebag full of tools. "I can take Flint with me."

"He's all right. He can hand me whatever I need and

help me measure." He smiled at Flint, now holding a hammer.

"Are you sure?" she asked. "I don't want him to be a bother."

"If he's anything like Billy, he won't be." He looked over the porch. "There are a few boards I'm going to take up first, measure, then fetch some lumber. I'll do the same with the back porch."

"At least let me get you a cup of coffee," she said. "I just put on a pot."

"Thank you, coffee would be nice." He took the hammer from Flint and began examining the porch again.

Sarah took Lacey's hand and returned to the kitchen. She got two cups and saucers from the hutch and put them on the table.

"Mama?"

"What, sweetheart?"

"Do you like Mr. Darling?"

Sarah stopped and looked at Lacey. "Excuse me?"

Lacey blinked like an owl. "Do you like him?"

Sarah knew that look. It meant she wanted something or was trying to play innocent. "I suppose. But I don't know him very well."

Lacey hugged Mrs. Winkle and began to weave back and forth. "Do you *think* you'll like him?"

Sarah reached for the coffee pot. "What sort of question is that, young lady?"

Lacey shrugged. "I was just asking. Cassie likes Conrad."

Sarah filled the cups. "And how do you know that?"

"Because Billy says he saw them kissing."

Sarah gasped. "Oh, my!"

"You mean you didn't know?" Lacey asked innocently.

"I'm trying to figure out how *you* know." Sarah returned the pot to the stove. "When did Billy tell you this?"

"Last night."

Sarah's mind raced. "Where were we last night?"

"We went to Captain Stanley's, remember?"

"Oh, yes, we had dinner with him." She picked up her cup, took a sip, then added a little sugar. "When did you see Billy?"

"He was outside playing while you and the captain were talking." Lacey went to the kitchen table, climbed onto a chair, and eyed the coffee cups. "Can I have some?"

"You know perfectly well you're too young for coffee. Speaking of which, leave mine alone. I have to take Mr. Darling his." She picked up the other cup and saucer and headed for the front door. Thankfully Lacey followed.

"Ma, guess what?" Flint said with wide eyes.

Sarah noticed his cheeks were pink and wondered what the two had been talking about. "What?"

"Mr. Darling says I can help with the whole project if

I'm a good worker." He grinned and looked at Mr. Darling, who was measuring one of the rotten boards.

"Did you?" she asked.

"I did. So far, he knows what all the tools are and asked a few good questions. I don't expect him to work like Billy did, but he would be handy to have."

"So long as you're sure." She gave Flint the look that said *you'd better behave*. "You'll do everything Mr. Darling says, is that understood?"

Flint saluted. "Yes, ma'am."

Mr. Darling chuckled. "He spends a lot of time with the captain, doesn't he?"

"Me too!" Lacey said and skipped across the porch to him. "What are you doing?"

"Measuring this board because I'm going to tear it out and replace it with a new one." He climbed to his feet, spied the cup and saucer in Sarah's hands and smiled. "That for me?"

"It is." She handed them to him.

Flint picked up the saddlebags. "This is heavy. You want me to carry it anywhere for you?"

Mr. Darling took a sip of coffee and smiled. "Young man, you're willing and able. But no, leave them on the porch."

"Okay." Flint let the saddlebags slide off his shoulder and land on the porch with a *thud*.

Sarah cringed. He was copying what he'd seen Mr. Darling do earlier. "I'm so sorry about that. You have to understand, children take you literally."

He took another sip of coffee and smiled. "I confess I haven't been around many children. Our family consists of all males except our mother. No sisters. So, none of us have any experience with children other than those in the village."

"Village?"

"Where ... we live," he said carefully. "Here you call them towns, there we say village."

"You talk funny," Lacey commented.

"It's called an accent," Mr. Darling said. "To me, *you* talk funny."

Lacey's face screwed up. "I do not."

"To me you do," he sang, then took another sip. "As much as I like having this conversation on our differing ways of speech, young miss, I must continue my work. Time is precious." He drained the cup and handed it and the saucer back to Sarah.

She took them, then shooed Lacey toward the door. "I need a few things from the general store. I'd better take Flint with me."

"But Ma ...," Flint whined.

"I don't mind if he stays," Mr. Darling said. "If you need to go, then go."

Sarah hesitated a moment, saw the hopeful look on Flint's face and relented. "Very well. He can stay. We'll be back soon." She left the porch, her heart skipping a beat. She wasn't sure if it was from the man's handsome looks or that she was leaving her son alone with him. All she knew was that she had a few more minutes to make up her mind on whether she trusted this man or not.

Irving ripped out another porch board and tossed it aside. As it turned out, the Widow Crawford returned and dragged poor Flint to town with her anyway. It was obvious she didn't trust him. He planned to remedy that as soon as he could. If he was to be the new Viscount Darlington, then he had to have all the tenants on the estate trusting him. If he could win the Widow Crawford and her children over, he had a shot with his father's tenants back home.

News would travel fast once they returned, and he wanted to be prepared to do his part. If Sterling did indeed remain in America, then he himself was going to be put through the wringer, as they say. And it wasn't going to be pretty. Mother would be very upset, take it out on Father, who in turn would take it out on him, since he was the next in line to inherit after Sterling and, in their father's eyes, should be able to take things like a man.

He ripped out another board and added it to the pile, measured it, scribbled down the measurements, then went on to the next. Once he pulled up all the rotten boards, he took a look at the fence going around the yard. A couple of posts would have to be replaced, along with at least a dozen or more pieces of fencing. The whole thing could do with paint besides.

Curious, he went around the back of the house to see that porch. He wasn't expecting a full clothesline, nor the old rickety table with a washtub on it and three baskets of dirty laundry. "My word, that poor woman." Hadn't Letty mentioned something about the Widow Crawford having to do what she could to get by?

"A laundress?" He shivered at the thought, then went to examine the porch. He also made a mental note to look at her hands the next time he saw her. To have to do other people's laundry so she could feed her children ... well, not even his family's tenants had to do that.

He found several boards that needed to be replaced on the back porch and returned to the front of the house to get his hammer. He'd pull them up, measure, write everything down, then ponder taking another look inside. He had yet to see the kitchen or the widow's bedroom.

Irving stopped halfway to the front and looked at the house's peeling paint. "Widow indeed. I suppose I should stop calling her that and refer to her as Mrs. Crawford." Problem was, she didn't look like a Mrs. Crawford. Miss Crawford maybe, but there were children, so he supposed ...

"Irving, here you are," Oliver said as he came around the side of the house. "I've been looking for you."

"And you've found me. What disaster brought you here?" He started for the front again.

"Why does my showing up have to equal a disaster?" Oliver trotted after him and beat him to the porch. "I came to assist you."

"I already have an assistant." He noted Oliver was blocking his path. "Kindly move out of the way."

Oliver sidestepped right. "Who's helping you? Wallis didn't say anything to me about it."

"Not you, Mr. Crawford is helping me." He picked up the saddlebag. "Young Mr. Crawford."

Oliver laughed. "Her child? He can't be more than five."

"Six, for your information. Practically a man around here."

"And what does that make Billy?" Oliver asked with a laugh.

Irving smiled. "An old man." He started down the porch steps. "Conrad says he sometimes has the disposition of one."

Oliver laughed again and followed him. "Where are you going?"

"I need a lot of lumber. But first I must wait for Mrs. Crawford to return from the general store. Then I'll take a good look around the house, make a full list, and get whatever I need to get this job properly started."

Oliver glanced at the house and back. "What have you done so far?"

"Not much. Ripped out a few rotten porch boards. How is Conrad coming along?"

"Cassie's house is almost done. Since Phileas is helping Conrad, I thought I'd help you."

"That's very thoughtful, Oliver, thank you."

Oliver took a sudden interest in the picket fence. "So what do you think about Conrad's declaration of love to Cassie?" He turned to face him. "Not to mention his becoming her deputy?"

Irving pinched the bridge of his nose. "I would think you can guess, dear brother. Am I jumping for joy over it? What happens if I were to fall in love with a fair maid of Apple Blossom?"

Oliver gave him a blank stare, then whistled. "Poor Phileas."

"Indeed, unless of course I decided to take the fair maiden back to England with me."

Oliver blinked a few times in confusion. "Wait a minute, what are you talking about? Has Sterling said something to you? He's not staying, is he?"

Irving secured his saddlebags then gave his horse a pat. "It's a possibility. We all know that."

"But you don't think Sterling is serious about it, do you? If he did, that would mean you ..." Oliver was wise enough to snap his mouth shut.

Irving took a calming breath. "Exactly. So is it any wonder I'm a little nervous?"

Oliver was too, as a shaky chuckle showed. "Wouldn't it be something if we all fell in love and none of us returned to England?"

Irving stared at him in shock a moment, then laughed. "Please don't jest."

Oliver ran a hand across the top of the fence. "Well, I was thinking of the worst-case scenario. Seeing as how I'm the youngest."

Irving sighed. "Good point." He looked at the road, saw no sign of the widow ... that is, Mrs. Crawford, then looked at the house. "I really need to get inside."

"Then why don't you?" Oliver asked. "You're here to work on it."

"Because she doesn't trust me, that's why." He returned to the porch steps and sat. Oliver joined him.

They sat in silence a few moments before they heard the giggles of children in the distance. "Sounds like they're returning," Oliver said.

"Good. I need to get some work done. This place is not in good shape."

"Mr. Crawford wasn't very good at repairing things?" Oliver inquired.

Irving sighed. "Somehow I don't think Mr. Crawford had the money or the inclination. I don't know which – perhaps both." He looked at the road as Mrs. Crawford and her children came into view. "I feel sorry for them, Ollie. There are piles of laundry in the backyard this woman is doing for people in town." He looked at his brother. "Our tenants live like kings compared to these three."

Oliver's face fell as he looked at the approaching trio. "Yet they look so happy."

"Yes, I've noticed. But they have so little."

Flint raced for the gate, came through and ran up the front walk. "Howdy! Which one are you?"

Oliver smiled. "You can call me Ollie. That's what my brothers do."

Flint's face screwed up. "Ollie? What kind of name is that?"

"Flint," Mrs. Crawford called from the gate. "Don't be rude."

"He's all right," Oliver said. "I just came by to see if my brother needed any help."

Flint jabbed himself with a thumb. "Hey, I'm helping."

"Flint!" his mother snapped. "What did I just say?"

Irving smiled at the boy. "He's fine, Mrs. Crawford. He's keen to help."

She took Flint by the shoulders and steered him toward the porch. "He's eager to best Billy Watson. You just wait."

Irving noticed the gunnysack she carried. It looked heavy. "Would you like me to take that in for you?"

"No, I can manage." She took Lacey's hand as the girl stared at Oliver with wide eyes. "Come along, sweetheart. We have cookies to bake."

"You're going to do some baking?" Irving said in surprise.

"Yes, I promised the children. Then I have some work left to do."

He didn't want to say anything about the laundry

behind the house, or that she should forget about baking cookies. Instead, he smiled and tipped his hat. "I tore up a few porch boards in the back. Be mindful of them. I'm going to get some lumber now. Oliver will help me carry everything back."

"Very well," she said, her eyes darting between them. "When you return, I should have some cookies made." She smiled and hurried into the house, closing the door behind her.

"Do you still want to go inside and look around?" Oliver asked.

Irving stared at the house a moment, then shook his head. "No, let's get what we need and return." *And don't forget to look at her hands*, he reminded himself. It would be a good indicator of how hard she had to work just to eat.

Chapter Three

C aptain Stanley and Billy ducked behind some bushes as Irving and Oliver left Sarah Crawford's house. "Where are they going?" Billy asked.

"My guess is, to get some things to fix the house." The captain peeked through the bushes and watched the men ride by. "They're heading back to town." He looked at Billy. "Now, remember what you're supposed to do?"

"Tell Flint and Lacey what you want *them* to do, while you keep Mrs. Crawford busy."

"Aye, lad. C'mon, let's go." Captain Stanley ducked back out of the foliage and onto the trail they'd been traversing. It ran parallel to the road, and he used it often while hunting rabbits and sea beasts.

"Captain Stanley?" Billy asked as they set off. "What if this doesn't work? Won't Flint and Lacey be disappointed?"

He stopped and turned to the boy. "Aye, which is why we must make sure it works. That poor widow needs a husband, and Flint and Lacey need a father. You want them to have one, don't you?"

"Oh, sure," Billy said. "It's just that this Mr. Darling isn't like the others." He scowled. "He's stuffy."

The captain's hands went to his hips. "Aye, that he is. Well, there's no help for it."

"Can we un-stuff him?"

The captain laughed. "If you can figure out how to do that, lad, then be my guest." He continued down the trail, Billy following. Once they found a break in the underbrush, they approached the Widow Crawford's house from up the road. He didn't want too many folks knowing he'd made the trail years ago, and so far, only the children did. It was one of the ways they cut to the apple orchards from the road into town. Captain Stanley built many such trails – some everyone knew about.

He knocked on the front door and waited, Billy beside him. When the door opened, he removed his cap and smiled. "Good afternoon, Sarah."

"Captain, what are you doing here?" She opened the door wide to let them in.

The captain stepped through, Billy on his heels. "I've brought you this. I seem to have a surplus of flour and sugar this month and thought you might like some." He held up a sack.

A hand went to her chest. "Bless you, Captain. I

could use both." She smiled. "The children and I were about to make cookies."

"Oh?" he said with raised eyebrows. He looked at Billy. "Looks like we came at the right time, lad."

Billy gave his signature grin. "Where are Flint and Lacey?"

"In the kitchen." She nodded that way.

Billy was off like a shot. Captain Stanley laughed. "That boy. I'm surprised he wanted to spend time with me today. He's been glued to that Conrad Darling all week."

"That's because the man had him working," she said. "Are they done?"

"I believe so. Now Mr. Conrad Darling has to act as Sheriff Cassie's deputy. We'll see how that goes."

She closed the door and led him into the kitchen. "I'm sure he'll do fine. Besides, it's only until they leave."

"What?" he said. "You mean you haven't heard?"

She took a cup and saucer from the hutch and set it on the table. "Heard what?"

"Cassie and Conrad ..."

"Oh, yes," she said. "They kissed." She eyed Billy. "So, you were an eyewitness?"

"I was," Billy said proudly. "It was a long kiss too."

The captain laughed. "You don't have to go into detail, lad."

Billy shrugged then whispered something into Flint's ear. The other boy nodded, grabbed Lacey's arm and the three headed for the back door.

"Where do you think you're going?" Sarah called after them.

"The backyard," Flint said. "We're going to make a scarecrow."

She sighed and nodded. "Very well, but do *not* use any of the laundry I'm working on."

"We won't," Billy said as he ushered his cohorts outside.

Captain Stanley smiled and sighed in satisfaction. His plan was moving along perfectly. "So, I hear you have one of them Englishmen helping you out now. What's he done so far?"

"Didn't you notice the missing porch boards?" She poured him a cup of coffee.

He grabbed the sugar bowl from the table and spooned some into his cup. "Can't say that I did. But I wasn't looking for them."

"You're lucky you didn't step in a hole." She poured herself a cup then took it and its saucer to the worktable. "I hope you don't mind if I continue what I was doing?"

"Of course not, lass. Make your cookies." He studied the dingy kitchen. "Caleb never did paint this when he said he would."

"No, he didn't," she stated.

The captain looked around some more. The kitchen was dreary and could use brightening up. The curtains were old, faded, and worn. One had a tear in the fabric, and it hung on its rod like a beggar's blanket. He could smell the years of cooking, especially the pancakes the widow always made for Flint and Lacey. He could also smell butter and various herbs and spices she used in her cooking. There was another odor, and he wondered if it was a skunk.

He took a sip of coffee and sighed. Caleb was a likable fellow but lacked ambition. The Englishman was a much better fit and would take better care of the place. Time to get to work. "Well, if Cassie and that Conrad fellow have something sparking between them, then good for them, I say."

She looked up from her work. "Really? Seems they made a hasty decision. How can anyone fall in love that fast?"

"Look at what happened to Letty, and now Cassie?" He tsk-tsked. "Don't hinder love, lass. When it blooms, sometimes it blooms fast. What if the same were to happen to you?"

She almost dropped the mixing bowl. "Me?" She laughed. "You're teasing."

"I'm not. If it could happen to Letty and Cassie, who knows whom love will strike next?"

She stirred her cookie dough. "Well, all I can say is it won't be me. I can't see it happening."

He sighed as his heart went out to her. Poor thing was scared to death. "And all I'm saying is keep an open mind. Who knows when a handsome young gentleman will pass this way again?"

"You mean six handsome gentlemen, don't you?" She brought a cookie sheet to the worktable and started dropping spoonfuls of dough onto it. "I do appreciate the work about to be done on my house. You know how badly it needs it."

"I do, lass, and I'm glad there's a young man willing to take care of things. I can do some work, but I'm not as young as I used to be."

She smiled at him. "I don't expect you to work on my house, Captain. You do so much for us already."

"As you and the children do for me. And I thank you for it."

"It's not so much as that," she said, putting the pan in the oven.

He shrugged. "Call me an old salt, but if it weren't for Flint and Lacey and yourself, I'd be a lonely captain indeed."

"Lonely?" she said with a laugh. "You're surrounded by the town's children wherever you go."

Captain Stanley smiled. It was true. "Well, a man likes to have a little adult conversation now and then."

She nodded in understanding and started to drop dough onto another sheet. He'd purchased the sheets for her in Virginia City a few months back. The ones she'd had were in sorry shape.

He looked past her at the open door to her bedroom. The door itself could do with a lick of paint, and the walls inside the room had been stripped back to bare whitewash, like the walls of an ancient castle. Maybe Caleb had started on the bedroom but never got to finish. He could also see an old desk in a corner with a stack of books on it but other than that, not much else.

"Something the matter?" she asked.

"No, nothing." He picked up his cup and wondered how Billy was faring with his mission. Flint and Lacey were to give him their report on what they had accomplished so far. He hoped Lacey didn't give anything away, but at least she was determined to see her mother happy. It was more than you could say for her mother.

By the time the first batch of cookies was done, the children had returned to the kitchen. The five talked, laughed, enjoyed their cookies, and whiled away the time until Mr. Darling returned. "Well, now that the lad is back," Captain Stanley said. "I should move along. I'll only be in the way."

Sarah left the table to answer the door. "You're welcome to stay if you wish, Captain."

"I've work to do, lass," he called after her, then bent to the children. "Well?" he hissed.

"They understand your orders, Captain," Billy said.

"Do you, Flint, Lacey?" He glanced at the parlor and back. "Hurry now, here he comes."

Lacey smiled. "Mama is supposed to fall in love with the Englishman."

"Right you are, young lady." He glanced at the parlor one last time.

"Which one was he again?" she asked. "I forgot already."

The captain facepalmed. Maybe this wasn't such a

good idea after all. "The one working on your house," he whispered.

"But there's two," she said.

He drew closer. "Irving."

"Oh, okay." Lacey hugged her doll. "We can do that."

Captain Stanley straightened. "See that you do." He smiled at the children, then headed for the back door.

Sarah glanced at her dress before she opened the door. She didn't know why she was concerned over how she looked. Maybe because Mr. Darling was so handsome. What would he think of her day dress and apron? The dress was ashen-gray cotton and clean enough, but old and faded. The bodice was plain with seams and stitched repairs along the hem, the sleeves, and the shoulders. The soap she'd used that morning for the laundry still lingered on her sleeves, mixed with the burnt odor of kerosene.

She didn't pay attention to such details earlier and shouldn't now. She opened the door. "You're back," she stated as Mr. Darling smiled. "The captain's here, but he's leaving." She pulled the door wide then turned around. There was no sign of the captain. She'd thought he was right behind her. "Now where did he go?"

Flint ran into the parlor. "The captain and Billy went out the back door."

Sarah sighed. "Well, that's the captain for you." She turned around. "You never know what he might do."

Mr. Darling entered smelling of cedar and roses, the natural aroma of his skin mixed with the comforting perfume of some cologne. He was a rather tall man with dark hair and blue eyes and wore a plain but clean dark suit. The top button of his black vest was undone, revealing a white shirt which wasn't overly starched or ironed. His brown leather boots were polished, and like his shirt, only enough to make them presentable. They still showed signs of wear.

Sometimes she wondered about the Englishmen. They were so well-mannered. Were all Englishmen this way? One would think they were highborn gentlemen instead of simple farmers.

"Is something the matter?" he asked. "You're, um, staring."

She blinked. "I'm sorry, I didn't realize …" She stuck her hands in her apron pockets. "I have cookies in the oven. If you'll excuse me." She hurried to the kitchen, cringing all the way. How could she let herself stare at him like that? What must he think of her now? Mercy, that was embarrassing. She took the next batch of cookies out of the oven and put in another.

Mr. Darling entered the kitchen, and she noticed for the first time that he was alone. "Where is your brother?"

"Oliver? We ran into Phileas and Conrad at the feed store. He helped me carry the lumber I needed over here and is off to Sheriff Cassie's house to help them with something."

"What happened to his helping you?" she asked, curious.

He eyed the cookies. "Conrad said that the sooner he got Cassie's house done, the sooner he could help me with yours." He shrugged. "I couldn't argue with that."

She glanced around her dreary little kitchen. "I see. Well, you have Flint, at least."

He smiled. "Speaking of which, where did he go?"

Sarah gasped and looked around. "Flint?"

He came running from her room. "Ma, do you have any tools?"

"What?"

"I need them to help Mr. Darling." Flint ran to him. "Can I hammer in the nails?"

Her shoulders slumped. "We have some of your father's old tools in the shed." She headed for the back door. "I'll have to fetch them."

"No need." Mr. Darling stepped toward her.

Sarah turned around and was almost nose to nose with him. Her heart skipped and she nodded. "Very well." She sidestepped around him to the worktable. "Would you like a cookie?"

"I admit, since coming to Apple Blossom, my admiration for the cookie has increased tenfold."

She laughed. "That's one way of saying it."

"What did you say?" Flint asked.

"I said I like cookies." He began to study the kitchen, then frowned. "Where is your daughter?"

She looked too, didn't see Lacey anywhere, and headed for the children's bedroom. "Lacey?"

"She's in there," Flint said. "She was putting Mrs. Winkle down for a nap."

Sarah reached the door, surprised Mr. Darling followed. "Oh, yes, it's about that time."

Mr. Darling's eyebrows shot up. "Mrs. Winkle?"

"Her doll," Sarah said. "She's never without it." She smiled. "Mrs. Winkle is very old and needs naps." She pushed open the door to the children's room. Not only was Mrs. Winkle taking a nap, but so was Lacey. She lay on her little bed, the doll in her arms, sound asleep. Poor Mrs. Winkle's left eye needed repairing again – it was about to fall off.

"She's adorable," Mr. Darling whispered behind her.

A chill went up her spine, and she had to remember to breathe. Mercy, if this kept up, she didn't know what she'd do. "Thank you. I think so too."

"Flint is an eager lad, and I'll try to teach him a few things. I'm afraid none of us are carpenters by trade, but we have had to help fix things around the, uh, farm."

"What you and your brothers are doing most of us can do too, we just don't have the time or, I'm ashamed to say for some of us, the inclination."

"Grief has a way of draining everything out of a person. I've seen it before."

She turned around. "Have you?"

"Yes. But time heals all things, as they say, and this too shall pass." He gave her a warm smile then took a few steps back. "Now, about that cookie?"

"Oh!" Sarah hurried past him to the kitchen, hoping he didn't think she was some scatterbrain that couldn't so much as keep track of her children. That wasn't the case at all. But he made her nervous. The only man to come to the house was the captain, and of course Rev. Arnold after Caleb was killed. The reverend saw as many folks as he could after the incident. Now it was the other way around. Folks were going to see him to take care of little things around his home and yard. The poor man was getting so old, he'd have to give up preaching sooner than later.

She put some cookies on a plate and set them on the table. "Help yourself." She returned to take the next batch out of the oven. "As soon as I have these baked, I have work to do. I'll be in the backyard if you need me."

"Very well," he said. "Flint and I will be in the front. Will our hammering wake Lacey?"

"Don't worry about her. That child can sleep through anything." She smiled and started removing the next batch of cookies to a second plate. She'd let them cool, then put them in the cookie jar.

Mr. Darling took a few, excused himself, then motioned Flint to follow. They returned to the front porch, leaving Sarah alone with her thoughts and freshly baked molasses cookies. She took one and enjoyed the chewy goodness of her first bite. If she wasn't careful, she could eat half a dozen. She realized she was hungry and hadn't made anything for lunch. She'd have to remedy that and looked at the clock on the hutch. She was running out of time – before she knew it, she'd be out of daylight to finish the laundry.

She hurried to complete her baking, then made a few sandwiches. Flint would want one, as would Lacey once she woke up. She wasn't sure if Mr. Darling brought any food with him or not. Thank Heaven she'd made bread yesterday.

Outside, she resumed her washing and started the next load. She hoped it didn't rain later as many of the clothes would be left on the line overnight. Clouds had dotted the sky off and on today and there was a light breeze. Sudden storms at this time of year were not uncommon, and she prayed one wasn't brewing. If the captain was still here, she'd ask what he thought. The man could read the weather like no one else she knew.

She was working on Mr. and Mrs. Smythe's laundry now. They were getting older, and sometimes Mrs. Smythe's hands pained her. Scrubbing laundry was one of those chores she disliked doing and didn't mind hiring Sarah to do it for her. Sarah liked working for them. They were kind and always nice to the children.

Her gaze drifted toward the front corner of the house where hammering had started. Judging from the consistent rapping, Mr. Darling oversaw the tool. If Flint had it, there'd be a *tap-tap*, followed by a cry of pain. Flint had terrible aim. She should have warned Mr. Darling but didn't think of it until now.

She took the opportunity to think about her little home and her current situation. If she worked hard and didn't lose any business, she could make it. The problem would be winter. How was she going to bear the cold? Her kitchen was too small to set up her washing and drying. She could hang clothes in the parlor, she supposed, but didn't want to do that unless she had to.

Her heart sank when she realized she was going to have to figure that out fast. The last thing she wanted was to catch her death of influenza. If something happened to her, what would happen to the children?

Sarah put her hand to her chest as her breaths came in rapid succession. She hated when this happened, and though it didn't very often, it still scared her. She tried to calm herself by running Mr. Smythe's denims up and down the scrub board very slowly and concentrate on the movement. After she took a few deep breaths, the spell passed. She closed her eyes and sent up a silent prayer that she wouldn't have another such attack until after Mr. Darling was done working on her house.

Chapter Four

Irving showed Flint the proper way to hold a hammer and a nail. He could tell by the gleam in his eye that Flint would hit first, aim later. As mending smashed fingers was not on Irving's to-do list, he took the extra time to make sure Flint handled the tool correctly. At some point he thought he heard the back door open and close. Was Mrs. Crawford returning to her piles of laundry?

He watched Flint organize a handful of nails, lining them up in neat rows. "Your mother is a laundress then?"

Flint gave him a blank stare, his mouth half-open. "A what?"

"She washes clothes for people." Irving took one of the nails and hammered it into place.

"Oh, that. Yes'm. She's been doing that for a spell." Flint pulled a few more nails out of the sack and lined them up too.

"She works hard," Irving stated.

Flint nodded. "She comes into the house all sweaty and has to change her dress." He picked up a nail. "Do you need another one yet?"

"Yes, thank you." Irving took it and placed it where he wanted on the board. "She must love you very much to work so hard."

Flint looked at him again. "Yes'm." He hung his head. "Sometimes I feel guilty for not getting work." He frowned. "But no one will hire me, except the captain. He lets me sweep the saloon."

Irving made a show of raising his eyebrows. "He does? At your age? What would your mother say?"

"She don't say anything on account she's usually cleaning the bar while I sweep. Lacey dusts."

Irving pounded the next nail in and pondered what the boy said. Did the captain pay Mrs. Crawford to clean for him? He still hadn't taken a good look at her hands, not the way he wanted. Was she working herself to the bone to feed her children? He hammered in another nail and smiled. "There, this one's done." He smiled at Flint. "You're a good assistant."

The boy smiled back. "Thanks!" He frowned again. "Do you think Billy's better?"

"To be honest, I wouldn't know. I've not worked with Billy. I only have my brother's word on the matter."

Flint nodded as he absorbed this. "Will you tell your brother I'm a good worker?"

45

Irving got to his feet to fetch another board. "Are you hoping it will get around to Billy?"

Flint blushed. "Maybe."

Irving laughed. "I'll do my best. But that means you'll have to do a good job. You wouldn't want me to give my brother a bad report on you."

"No, sir." Flint shook his head. "I'll never hear the end of it."

Irving sighed. "It's not a competition, you know. But I suppose a little doesn't hurt." He went to his pile of boards and brought another to the porch. "Will you excuse me for a minute?"

"Sure." Flint reached for the hammer. "Can I nail in the next one?"

"Wait for me. In fact ..." Irving held out his hand. "The hammer, if you please."

"Aw, gee." Flint handed him the tool.

"I'll be right back. Why don't you bring a few more boards onto the porch?"

"Okay." The boy headed for the pile in the yard.

His curiosity getting the best of him, Irving headed around to the back of the house. Once around the corner, he stopped. Mrs. Crawford was bent over the washtub, scrubbing a piece of clothing. Her entire body moved with the effort, and he noticed her hair coming loose from its pins. She stopped at one point, wiped her brow with the back of her hand, then got back to work.

For some reason the image disturbed him. It wasn't as if he was repelled by it – on the contrary, his heart went out to her, and he wanted to gently push her aside and take over. She looked tired now, and he noticed how thin she was. In fact, he was noticing a lot of things: the state of her dress, the way she had the laundry lined up to be washed much like Flint aligned the nails to be used. She had things organized but was only one person.

Irving retraced his steps to the front. Flint had a pile of boards stacked neatly by his rows of nails. "Very good. You work like your mother."

"What?" He made a face. "I don't do laundry."

"No, but you're organized like she is." He prepared to hammer in another board and explained to Flint what to do. "Now try to pound in a nail." He handed him the hammer.

Flint took it, licked his lower lip then got into position. Irving sent up a silent prayer that any screams of pain didn't bring his mother running.

Flint raised the hammer and brought it down hard. "Hey, I hit it!"

Irving managed a nervous laugh. "You did. Now do it again. Be careful now."

Flint did as before and hit the nail square on the head. Irving released the breath he'd been holding. So far, so good. It would be slow going at this rate but at least the boy would have gotten one nail in place. He'd do two, then let Flint do the last.

Irving watched Flint closely as he pounded the nail one slow whack at a time and wondered how Mrs. Crawford was doing with all that laundry. It looked like several days' worth, and he pondered lending her a hand. He could have the porch boards replaced quickly enough. In fact, so long as Flint didn't smash a finger, he'd bring an extra hammer tomorrow and have him nail the new fencing together. A section, anyway. That would give the boy some bragging rights. As far as Irving knew, Billy hadn't done any work on Sheriff Cassie's fence.

When Flint was done, Irving took the hammer and got to it. By the time they were done with the front porch, over an hour had gone by. Now they could move to the back.

When they carried the lumber around the house, he noticed Mrs. Crawford wasn't there. "Where's your mother?"

"Probably in the house. She needs to rest now and then." Flint reached the back porch and dumped his load on the ground. "Want a cookie?"

"Sure." What he really wanted was to check on Mrs. Crawford. She was thin, almost frail, and he wondered if she could do the amount of work she was trying for.

Inside they found her sitting at the kitchen table, a cup of coffee in her hands. "Oh, hello," she said. "Done already?"

Irving looked her over. "We still have the back porch." His eyes fixed on her hands. They were rough and moved slowly as if each muscle ached. From the way her fingers curled around the mug, Irving figured the joints themselves ached deeply. Her movements reminded him of an old woman whose body was bowing to age.

"Is something wrong?" she asked.

He blinked. "No, nothing." He looked away. "Flint offered me a cookie."

She eyed her son. "Flint, what did I tell you earlier?"

Flint looked chastised. "Not to eat all the cookies. But Mr. Darling looked like he needed one."

She sat back in her chair and sighed. "Get the jar."

Irving noticed the plate of cookies she had out earlier was gone. "He likes his cookies?"

She set her cup down. "You have no idea." She used the table to push herself out of her chair. "Would you like some coffee?"

"I can get it." He headed for the stove. "Sit, rest." Because if she didn't, he thought she might drop from exhaustion. Questions began to form: did she get enough to eat? Was she going without to make sure her children were fed? And of course, what could he do about it? Should he do anything about it? He was already fixing things around here and had only so much time to do it. Maybe he'd speak to Sterling ...

"Here you go, Mr. Darling." Flint handed him three cookies.

"Thank you." Irving took them and set them on the worktable.

"Flint Michael Crawford," his mother cried. "One cookie is enough."

"But Ma, we're working men. We need our strength."

49

He took a huge bite of the cookie in his hand as he put the other hand behind his back.

She rolled her eyes. "You've been spending too much time with Billy."

"How can I?" Flint said. "He's *always* working. Can you imagine how many cookies he gets?"

Irving burst out laughing. "I say, you *have* been spending a lot of time with Billy. You're starting to sound just like him."

Flint smiled mischievously and ran out the back door.

Mrs. Crawford buried her face in her hands. "Oh, that boy."

Irving went to her. "Here now, are you all right?"

She looked at him and crossed her arms. "Yes, it's just that Flint is trying so hard to be the man of the house and it worries me."

Irving glanced at the back door. "I see. And he views Billy Watson as having achieved that goal?"

"I think so. Difference is, Billy still has his father." She started for the coffee pot.

Irving gently took her arm and steered her back to the table. He looked at her cup. It was empty. "Would you like some more?"

"Yes, I would." She sat. "Thank you."

He smiled then fetched the pot. After pouring her another cup, he refilled his own, and sat across the table from her. "So, tell me, Mrs. Crawford. How long have you been a laundress?"

Sarah stared at him. Why would he ask such a thing? "Well, I ... needed ..." She stopped and looked at her cup. "Caleb, my husband, and I had a little money put away. But it's running out." She swallowed hard as her cheeks heated. "I have to do whatever I can to get by." She looked at him and hoped he'd leave well enough alone.

"I understand," Mr. Darling said. "I'm sorry you and so many others have suffered. We all are."

"Is that why you're helping us?" She ran her finger over the rim of her cup.

"It's one of the reasons." He stared at her a moment, and she caught the compassion in his eyes. Her heart responded and tears threatened. She'd been strong for her children but hadn't done so well being strong for herself. She missed Caleb. He was company, someone to talk to. Were they in love with each other? No, not really. But between the two of them, they could survive, and that's what mattered to them both.

Now he was gone, and she wasn't doing such a great job of surviving. But she had the children to think of and had to take care of them as best she could. Sometimes she wondered how much they missed their father. He had been distant around them, as if he wasn't quite sure what to do with them.

"There's a lot of work here," Mr. Darling said, pulling her from her reverie. "I'll get everything outside done first, the porches and fence. Then I'll start on the inside." He studied the kitchen. "What color would you like this?"

She looked around. "Color? In a kitchen?"

"Yes, kitchens where I come from are very ..." He smiled. "... colorful."

She smiled back. "Are they?"

He glanced around. "A light green perhaps?"

"Green? For a kitchen?"

"Our kitchen at home is green." He took a sip of coffee, made a face, then added some sugar.

A chill went up her spine. She still didn't know what to make of him and wasn't about to try. The sooner he got his work done the better. Then she could go on with her life and figure out what to do for winter. She still wasn't sure how she'd manage it.

"Do you need help?" He stared at his coffee then looked at her. "With the laundry?"

Sarah gasped. "No, of course not."

He looked her in the eyes. "You have several baskets out there. When is it due to be delivered?"

She swallowed. "Tomorrow."

"Then you do need help," he stated. He took another sip of coffee. "I've never done much laundry, but if you show me, I'm sure I'll pick it up in no time."

She looked confused. "Y-you want to help me wash clothes?"

"So you get done in time, yes. Is that so strange?"

She laughed. "Well, yes. It is."

He shrugged. "My brothers and I decided to stay and

help you people out. So what if that includes doing a little laundry?"

She didn't know what to say. His offer to help with such a lowly task made her wonder if he was joking. But the look in his eyes said otherwise. They were deep and laden, as if he were full of a wisdom she'd never possess, like a grandfather filled with cares of the world. In them, she saw a soul who had seen much more than she could have ever imagined. A reminder at how small her life had become.

"Well, Mrs. Crawford?" he said. "What do you say? Will you teach me?"

She laughed and hoped she didn't sound like she was on the verge of hysterics. "There's not much to learn. And I must admit, with two of us working the job would get done much sooner."

"Then let's get started." His face lit up, and he smiled at something behind her.

She turned as Lacey entered the kitchen rubbing her eye with one hand and holding Mrs. Winkle with the other. "Mama, where's Flint?"

"He's outside eating a cookie." She ran a hand through her daughter's hair. "Would you like one?"

"Yes, please." She held up her doll. "So would Mrs. Winkle."

Sarah sighed. "Does she now?"

"She does." Lacey rubbed her other eye then leaned against her.

Sarah hugged her, then got up and headed for the

small larder. "Would you like another, Mr. Darling?"

"No, thank you. Three was enough for me."

She got a cookie for Lacey, one for herself, and returned. "Mr. Darling is going to help me do laundry. That means you and Flint will have to behave yourselves until we're done."

"We will, Mama." Lacey took the cookie she offered. "You'll see."

They finished their coffee, ate their cookies then went outside. Mr. Darling was quiet, and she wondered if he was regretting his offer to help. She'd have him rinse and wring what she'd washed already. Then Lacey and Flint could help him hang the clothes on the line.

Outside Flint was stacking and restacking the new porch boards. "Young man," Mr. Darling said. "We have a new job."

Flint grinned. "Do we get to pull up porch boards?"

"No, we get to do laundry," Mr. Darling announced.

"What?" Flint's face screwed up. "But why?"

"Because your mother can use the help." He went to the table with the washtub. "Your orders, madam?"

She smiled. "Are you English always so formal about everything?"

He cocked his head as if thinking. "Yes." He smiled. "What would you have me do?"

She pointed to the basket of wet laundry at his feet. "Those need rinsing. I use that washtub over there."

"Very good." He picked up the basket and carried it to the tub she had on top of the chopping block. "So the idea is to rinse, wring them out, then hang them up."

"Yes. They'll dry the rest of the afternoon and this evening. I'll iron them tomorrow morning." She joined him at the tub and took his hand in hers. She was surprised how large it was. "You'll be able to wring the fabric out better than me or the children ever could."

He looked into her eyes a moment. "I'd say you're right. No wonder it takes so much time to launder clothes."

"Indeed, Mr. Darling." She returned to the washtub and scrub board. "I'm going to heat some water. The clothes are easier to wash when the water's a little warm."

"Of course," he said. "Do you need any help with that?" He stood at the ready.

Sarah smiled at his willingness to help. "No, thank you." She headed for the porch, her smile still in place. No one had shown her kindness like this except the captain, and he never offered to help do laundry.

She filled the kettle and set it on the hottest part of the stove. While she waited for the water to heat, she watched Mr. Darling and the children work on the pile of washed laundry. Flint and Lacey dunked the clothes into the tub a few times, then Mr. Darling wrung out each piece and hung it on the clothesline.

She'd better remove the clothes she'd hung up earlier. Considering the warm day, they should be dry by now. She joined him at the clothesline with an empty basket. "Here, I'll take these inside."

He attached a pair of denims to the line with two wooden clothespins. "I shall forever have an appreciation for those that do my laundry."

"That would be your mother?"

"Erm, no. We, um, may be farmers, but we have some household help. There are so many of us, you see ..."

"Oh, yes, of course." She smiled and ran her hands over a few pairs of Mr. Featherstone's trousers. They seemed dry enough, so she removed them from the line. "Does your mother cook?"

"Oh, um," he hedged. "On occasion."

She pulled one of Mr. Featherstone's shirts off next. "You have a cook too?"

"Mmm."

So, his family had a maid and a cook. Well, maybe it was normal where he came from. Especially if the Darlings' farm was as big as it sounded.

She finished taking Mr. Featherstone's things off the line and carried the basket into the house, then brought the kettle outside and dumped it into the washtub. After refilling the kettle at the pump, she lugged it inside and set it on the stove again. By the time she returned outside, Mr. Darling was at the washtub, fingering the scrub board. "So, tell me what to do, and I'll take care of this for you."

Sarah gaped at him, looked at the empty basket by the other washtub and smiled. "Um, all right." She proceeded to show him how to scrub a pair of denims, feeling a little awestruck.

Chapter Five

The last of the laundry now washed and hanging on the line, Irving breathed a sigh of relief. "Flint, we have just enough time to pull up those rotten boards on the back porch."

Flint sighed in exasperation. "About time. Where's the hammer?"

Irving arched an eyebrow. "Didn't you have it last?"

The boy's face fell. "Oh, yeah."

"Best find it then, eh?"

Flint nodded and started searching.

Mrs. Crawford smiled at Irving and wiped her hands on her apron. "Thank you. I never could have finished this early. Now I can start supper."

Irving studied her a moment. She looked tired, her hair was falling from its pins, and her apron was drenched. Did she have the energy to cook? "I say, but why isn't there a café or restaurant in this town?"

She shrugged. "No call for it. Not enough people come through."

"We did, but we have the dining room at the hotel. Don't you ever want to sit at a table somewhere and have someone else do the cooking?"

She stared at him a moment, then let loose what he presumed was a laugh. More of a cackle, really. "Who would run it? And where would we put it? In case you haven't noticed, Mr. Darling, we have more people leaving Apple Blossom than coming."

"Still, it's a thought." He picked up a laundry basket of dried clothes. "Where would you like these?"

"My room. The ironing board is in there." She started for the house.

He followed. "I'll be right back, Flint."

"Found it!" Flint grinned and held the hammer up.

"Good. When I come back, I'll show you how to pull up a board with it." He went into the house and saw Mrs. Crawford leaning against the dry sink. "Are you all right?"

She looked at him, smiled and nodded. "Of course. Just a little tired." She stepped back, took a deep breath and glanced around the kitchen. "I'd best get to work."

He held up the basket. "Your room?"

"Oh, yes, let me take that." She took it from him and disappeared through a door near the pantry.

Since the door was now wide open, he stood on the threshold and took a peek. "My word."

Mrs. Crawford blushed deep red. "I told you my house wasn't much."

Irving took in the darkened room. Though it looked clean, it smelled of wood rot and something he couldn't put his finger on. Curious, he stepped inside, the floorboards creaking and groaning with his weight.

"Careful," she warned. "This side of the house isn't the best."

"I ... can see that. Great Scott, you're lucky the floor hasn't caved in."

She looked downward. "I know. I'm afraid it's only a matter of time."

He heard the strain in her voice, saw the worry in her eyes, and stepped closer. "Don't worry, Mrs. Crawford. There are six of us. We'll see what we can do."

Another cackle. "I'm afraid there's not much you can do other than replace the entire floor. I don't expect that."

"We'll discuss it. What happens if your floor were to fall apart in winter?"

She shuddered. "Please, I can't think about that right now." She hurried past him to the kitchen.

He took one last look at the floor, sighed and followed. He'd speak to his brothers over dinner. Speaking of which, he'd best get on with the back porch.

When he entered the kitchen, Mrs. Crawford was taking a pot from a shelf and setting it on the stove. "What are you going to make?"

She looked away. "Some broth and ..."

"Tell you what," he cut in. "Put that pot away and come back to the hotel with me. Dora always makes too much food. It's become apparent that the woman can't count. She thinks there's at least ten of us." He stepped toward her. "After dinner, I'll escort you and the children home."

She gave him a blank stare, as if she couldn't believe what he was saying.

"It's just a meal, my good woman. And a little social-izing." He smiled for good measure.

Her hand went to her mouth, and she turned away.

Irving drew in a breath. "While you're deciding, Flint and I will take care of the rotted boards on the back porch. I'll return for your answer then." He left the kitchen and rejoined Flint.

"About time," the boy griped. "Now show me how to tear these up."

"*Take* them up, you mean," Irving corrected. He glanced at the kitchen window. Mrs. Crawford was still by the stove from what he could see. Staring at it worriedly. It was dinner he offered, yet she acted like he'd asked her to hand over the deed to her house.

He got to work and let Flint try his hand at pulling up a board. The boy got the first nail out, then the second. The third wasn't so easy and he needed help, but he was getting the hang of it.

Lacey was nowhere to be seen, but after a moment or two, Irving heard her inside the house with her mother. He had a sudden image of the child holding a new doll and his heart warmed. Hmmm, he'd have to investigate that.

While they were pulling up the last board, Mrs. Crawford stepped onto the porch wearing a faded blue frock that hugged her small frame and had donned a matching bonnet. Her shawl was black and frayed and, frankly, Irving didn't care. She had accepted his invitation. It was all that mattered.

"Flint," she said. "We're going to town to have dinner with Mr. Darling and his family. Change your shirt and wash up."

Lacey joined them on the porch. She, too, was wearing a different dress. Like her mother's it was a faded blue, and Irving wondered if it was cut from the same bolt of cloth. He also noticed it wasn't as faded and worn as her mother's. "Is it time to go, Mama?"

"Not yet," Mrs. Crawford said. "We have to wait for Flint."

Flint got up and ran into the house without a word. Irving smiled. "Do they like going to town?"

"Oh, yes. Especially Alma's store."

"Sometimes Mama buys us a piece of candy," Lacey informed him.

He smiled. She was clutching her doll, Mrs. Winkle, and he saw once again in his mind's eye, Lacey holding a new one. Hmmm, did Alma have any dolls in stock?

"Flint will be right out," Mrs. Crawford said. "Can I help you put away your tools?"

He smiled. "I can do it." He gathered the old nails

and rotten boards and carried them to the front of the house. When he returned, he took the hammer and stuck it in his back pocket.

Flint returned wearing a different shirt that, like his mother and sister, was made of the same blue cloth. Was it their Sunday best? He hadn't paid much attention to them the day he and his brothers attended services. All eyes had been on Letty and Sterling. Tomorrow was Sunday, and he wondered if he'd see the three wearing their current clothes. "Are we ready?" Flint asked.

Irving looked into Mrs. Crawford's eyes. There was a hint of dullness in them, as if she'd fought a great battle and lost. If there was a doctor in town, he'd insist she see him, but as it was, Apple Blossom had nothing to offer in that regard. Pity. "Come," he said softly and nodded toward the front of the house. "The children can ride my horse."

Flint jumped up and down. "Yeehaw!"

"Flint Michael Crawford," his mother warned. "Calm yourself."

"Aw, Ma," the boy whined.

Irving felt a tug on his pants leg. It was Lacey. "Yes?"

She smiled. "Can Mrs. Winkle ride your horse?"

He bent to her. "So long as she doesn't race him down the street."

She smiled. "Mrs. Winkle would never. She's too much of a lady."

Irving patted the doll on the head. "I'm glad to hear

it, Mrs. Winkle." He smiled at Mrs. Crawford. "Shall we, then?"

"Yes, thank you." She started for the front of the house.

He took one last look at the sorry structure and exhaled. This was going to be a lot more work than he'd thought, but they couldn't leave her with a floor about to fall apart. Even if Captain Stanley tried to help, he was only one man, and Irving wasn't sure how capable he was at carpentry. Not that his brothers and himself were, but they'd helped with enough repairs to tenants' roofs and other things while growing up to give them some skills. Father wanted them to learn how to earn their tenants' respect and respect them in return.

Irving helped the children onto Patch, took the reins and began leading him down the road.

"Your hammer," Mrs. Crawford said. "It's still in your pocket."

He smiled, stopped Patch, and put the hammer into his saddlebag. "Thanks."

She looked at the ground. "You're welcome."

Unable to help himself, he put a hand on her shoulder, and she lifted her face to his. "Everything's going to be all right. We'll fix the floor."

She swallowed. "I ... it's too much."

"No, it's not. Between the six –" He glanced at Flint. "– seven of us, we can get it done in no time."

She didn't say anything at first. Just bit her lip and looked at him. "We'll discuss it later."

Irving nodded. If he had his way, they'd discuss more than her floor. She was vulnerable, dare he say a little lost? It tore his heart out. But what could he do about it in what little time he had left in this place?

Sarah wasn't sure what to say on the walk to town. The children giggled and laughed atop Mr. Darling's horse. Lacey clung to the saddle horn with one hand while Flint held onto her with both of his. Mr. Darling walked beside the horse and commented on their unceasing amusement.

"They'll laugh themselves right off him if they're not careful," she said.

He smiled at her. "They're having fun. Besides, I notice neither is letting go."

She smiled back, then noticed Flint pointing at something on the side of the road. She looked but saw nothing. "It's a nice evening."

"Indeed, it is," he said. "Warm and peaceful." He made a face at Flint and Lacey. "Except for you two. Whatever are you laughing at?"

"You!" Lacey cried.

"Me?" Mr. Darling said in mock surprise. "What did I do?"

"Nothing," Flint giggled. "You have a beetle in your hair."

Mr. Darling stopped and looked at her. "Do I?" He bent slightly so she could see.

Sarah smiled, then gasped. "My goodness, look at the size of it!"

"What?!" He quickly brushed at his hair. The beetle flew off and landed on the dusty road. "It's as big as a tree!"

Flint and Lacey flew into hysterics again.

"You could have warned me," he said, shaking a finger at them.

"He was going for a ride," Lacey giggled.

Mr. Darling ran his fingers through his hair. "He was nesting. Where's my hat?"

"I'm sorry," Sarah said. "You must have left it at the house."

"Dash it all, I did. Well, no help for it." He turned to the children. "If another beetle is brave enough to land on my head, inform me of it immediately."

The children laughed.

He sighed and turned to her. "I don't think they're taking me seriously."

She shook her head. "I'm afraid not."

"Well." He tugged at his vest. "You can't trust anyone these days. You try to keep your hair free from insects and for what?" He turned back to the children. "I'll remember your refusal the next time I see something crawling in *your* hair."

Flint and Lacey stopped laughing. "What?" Lacey said weakly. "But what if it's a big ugly spider?"

Mr. Darling gave them a pouty look. "Too bad."

Lacey gasped. "Mama!"

"He's joking," she said.

"Am I?" Irving laughed maniacally then continued down the road.

Flint laughed. "Aw, he's joking. He wouldn't let a spider crawl on you, Lace."

She twisted around to look at him. "Are you sure?"

Flint gave her a curt nod. "He's not a villain. He only tries to sound like one."

Mr. Darling grinned. "Clever boy."

Sarah smiled at his soft voice. She liked his accent and enjoyed talking with him, even when the conversation was uncomfortable.

She sighed as she thought of her bedroom floor. Would the Darlings start on her floor, see it as too much work and quit? She hoped not, but it was a possibility. She hated asking for help and had to bat down her guilt every time he talked about what the house needed. She knew it was a lot, but there wasn't much she could do about it on her own either. She had neither the strength, nor the funds, nor the tools. Caleb had a few, but a rusty saw and a hammer with a loose head wasn't going to do much.

When they reached town, a few folks were still out and about and smiled at them as they passed. Seemed everyone knew it was her turn to have her place worked on by the Englishmen, and most were probably relieved they weren't the ones doing it. Everyone was so wrapped up in their own lives and grief after the incident, she couldn't ask for help. It just didn't seem right.

When they got to the hotel Mr. Darling tied his horse to the hitching post, then helped the children down. "Now mind your manners at the table and be sure to thank Miss Jones for a lovely meal."

"We will," Lacey said with a smile. Flint took her hand and led her into the hotel.

Sarah watched them go. "You're very good with them, you know that?"

He shrugged. "To tell you the truth, I've not been around many children. Not for some time at least."

"Well, you'll make a good father one day." She headed for the hotel doors.

Mr. Darling hurried past, opened one, and nodded as she entered.

Inside they went to the dining room where the other brothers were already seated and speaking with Flint and Lacey. "Let's get some extra chairs," Sterling, the oldest, said.

Sarah wasn't sure she could remember all their names. "Good evening," she managed. "I hope you don't mind your brother inviting us to dine with you."

"It's no trouble," Dora said as she came out of the kitchen. She set a platter of fried chicken on the table. "Sarah, would you mind helping me?"

"Not at all." She turned to Flint and Lacey. "Behave."

Flint rolled his eyes then took the chair Sterling fetched for him.

Sarah followed Dora into the kitchen with a heavy sigh. "What's the matter?" Dora asked.

"Nothing, I'm just tired."

"It was nice of Irving to invite you; I want to hear all about your day." She handed her a bowl of mashed potatoes. "Careful, they're hot."

She took them, and she liked how the bowl's heat seeped into her hands. "Believe it or not, Mr. Darling helped with the laundry."

Dora stopped transferring green beans from a pot into another bowl. "He did? Well, is there nothing these men won't do?" She smiled at her. "I'm glad they're working on your place, Sarah, I really am." She spooned the rest of the beans into the bowl. "You know, you might consider selling it and moving into the Cutters' old house."

She shook her head. "And live next to the Featherstones? Besides, who would buy my place?"

"I don't know, but you should at least think about it. The children would be closer to their friends, and you wouldn't have to haul laundry back and forth the way you do. Besides, I bet you'd get more business."

She thought a moment. What Dora said made sense. "I still don't know who would buy my place."

"Maybe the captain can get the word out. He goes to Bozeman and Virginia City often enough."

She nodded. "True. I'll speak to him about it."

Dora smiled and nodded at the kitchen door. "Let's get this food on the table. The men look hungry."

"You're sure it's no trouble our being here?"

"We're honored you're joining us. Now let's eat."

Sarah followed her into the dining room and set the potatoes on the table. Her Mr. Darling went to an empty chair, smiled at her then pulled it out. She blushed, made her way around the table and sat.

"Looks good, doesn't it?" he said near her ear as he scooted her chair in.

A delicious thrill went up her spine and she blinked a few times. "Yes," she whispered, then cleared her throat. "Yes."

He bent closer. "I heard you the first time."

She blushed to her toes and quickly put her napkin in her lap. Good grief, did she just think of him as "her" Mr. Darling? She watched him go around the table to an empty seat and sit. As soon as he did, Phileas looked around the table, then made a show of clasping his hands in front of him. She did too, then nodded to Flint and Lacey to do the same.

"Dear Lord," Phileas said. "Bless this food to our bodies – that includes the extra ones – and may we achieve what we've set out to do. Amen."

She opened her eyes and looked at him, then the rest of the Darlings. There was Sterling the oldest. Oliver sat next to him, then Phileas. Dora was on his other side next to Flint. Then there was the brother whose name she couldn't remember – William, Wilbur, something like that. Then Lacey, herself, Conrad, and finally Irving. The man helping her.

Sarah looked at him and their eyes locked. It was the strangest sensation, not being able to look away, but here she was, her eyes fused with his and the mashed potatoes heading her way. In that moment, she wasn't sure which she wanted more, to keep gazing at Irving Darling or take the potatoes when they finally reached her.

Chapter Six

Come Monday morning, Captain Stanley and his faithful crew gathered in their usual meeting spot. "Now hear this," he bellowed. "I want your reports, then we'll begin making plans."

Lacey raised her hand. "What plans?"

"That remains to be seen," Captain Stanley said. "It all depends on what you have to report."

"Ohhh."

Jandy Brighton raised her hand. "I don't have anything to report."

The captain thought a moment. "That's because I didn't give you an assignment." He scratched his head. "Or did I?"

Billy stood and snapped to attention. "Permission to speak, Captain?"

"Permission granted." Captain Stanley sat on a crate and pulled his pipe out of a pocket.

"I've successfully completed my mission," Billy said. "Sheriff Cassie and Conrad Darling kiss when they think no one's looking."

"Excellent work, Billy." The captain lit his pipe and took a few puffs. "Flint, Lacey, you have your work cut out for you. But I plan to help."

Flint stood and saluted. "Aye, Captain. Our work has already begun. I'm helping our Mr. Darling work on the house just like Billy helped his Mr. Darling."

Lacey raised her hand again. "Do I get a Mr. Darling?"

"You already have one," Flint said next to her.

"But I don't want to share," Lacey whined. "I want my own."

"There's plenty of Darlings to go around," the captain said. "But the one you and your brother have is a little different. He's a practical sort from what I've observed. In fact, I'm not sure he has a romantic bone in his body. We'll have to do something about that."

"But what?" Flint asked.

Billy turned to him. "Just make sure he and your ma talk a lot. That helps. And take them fishing."

"Now hold on, lad," Captain Stanley said. "What worked for your Mr. Darling might not work for theirs. Yours was a flirt to begin with. I'm surprised he didn't kiss Cassie sooner." He took another puff on his pipe then looked Flint and Lacey in the eyes. "Now hear this, you two. If we're going to pull this off, you're going to need some help. We need to put them in a situation where they have no choice but to speak to each other about something other than your mother's house. Let me think ..."

Lacey raised her hand again. "Captain, what's a flirt?"

He sighed. "I'll explain later."

Alexander, Jandy's younger brother, raised his hand. "Do I get a Mr. Darling?"

"All in good time, Alex. Right now, we've got to work on the one called Irving." He thought a moment more before a smile formed on his lips. "I think I've got it."

"Got what?" Lacey asked.

"You two get your mother to come to the saloon tomorrow night." He left the crate and began to pace. "I'll invite Mr. Darling to dinner, see, and then the three of us will slip away after the meal, leaving your mother alone with him."

"But what are we going to do?" Lacey asked as she waved a fly away from Mrs. Winkle.

"We'll take a walk or something. The point is to give them a chance to be alone for a time."

Billy smiled. "That ought to do it."

The captain nodded. "It's a start. Anyone have any other ideas?" He looked over his students who were shrugging and exchanging the same look of confusion. He was asking too much of them, but one never knew. One of the older children might come up with an idea.

"Have they picked apples together yet?" Cheyenne Tate asked. She was twelve.

"Not that I know of," Captain Stanley said. "Good idea, though."

Ten-year-old Aubrey Lewis, who like Cheyenne had been quiet all this time, raised her hand. "Have they taken a walk together yet?"

"Flint?" The captain said.

He shrugged. "We all walked to town then back home Saturday night."

"That's a no." The captain returned to his crate and sat. "You two figure out how to get your mother to the saloon tomorrow night, and I'll take care of the rest, is that understood?"

"Aye, aye, Captain," Flint and Lacey said.

He arched an eyebrow and looked at the others. "As for the rest of you, keep an eye on Jean, Etta, and Dora."

"What do you have planned for them?" Jandy asked. At thirteen, she was the oldest.

The captain laughed. "What do you think, lass? They're perfect for the other three brothers. I just have to figure out who to pair up with whom."

"How do you do that?" Lacey held up her doll. "Mrs. Winkle wants to know too."

Captain Stanley winked. "Trade secret." He rubbed his hands together. "Now, on to your lessons."

The children groaned in protest. "We like match-making better," Billy said.

"So do I," said the captain. "But matchmaking's hard if you don't know how to read, write, or do your numbers."

The children looked at each other and shrugged. Captain Stanley didn't mind – after all, they were too young to understand the ways of love. But they did understand what it was like to be with two happy people watching over them. He would give that to those that needed it most right now. Namely, Sarah Crawford

Irving and Oliver moved Sarah's parlor furniture into the front yard. It was decided at dinner the other night that she should be on a first name basis with him and his brothers since Dora, Jean and Letty already were. He noticed Sarah still called him "Mr. Darling" in church yesterday, but that was okay. Maybe he'd have better luck today getting her to use his Christian name.

"Paint or wallpaper?" Oliver asked.

Irving stared at the house. "I'm not sure. To be honest, if we had the time, I'd like to build her a new cabin."

"Dora mentioned a house in town that would suit Sarah and her children well. Did she say anything to you about it?"

"No. What house is this?"

"It belonged to one of the families that left not long ago. There's also an apartment over the millinery shop. Dora also said Sarah is a good seamstress."

"Is she? I was only aware she does laundry for people, including the Featherstones."

Oliver shuddered. "Poor woman."

Irving nodded and headed for the house. They were going to take a good look at the floorboards and decide if any needed replacing. So far things seemed to be intact in the parlor, but one never knew.

Inside, he went to the area where the sofa had sat and checked out the boards. Nothing spongy, everything solid. Good. "If Sarah does decide to sell this place, then the least we can do is help fix it up. Either way there's work that needs to be done. To me it's the same work whether she stays or goes."

"You're right, of course," Oliver said. "But you might mention it."

"I will." He looked at the kitchen, knowing Sarah was in the backyard washing clothes. "I wonder if she's ever tried her hand at hat making."

Oliver shrugged. "Never hurts to ask. It would be better than doing other people's laundry, don't you think?"

"Quite. The poor woman looks like she's worked herself to the bone."

"We noticed," Oliver said with a hint of guilt. "We talked about her after you left to escort her home the other night."

"Anyone can see it, brother. I don't know what to do about it other than fix this place up." Irving went to a corner of the room and checked the floorboards there, then the opposite corner. Everything was good. "How would you like to crawl under the house?"

Oliver's eyes popped wide. "Surely you jest."

"You're a bit thinner than I, Ollie – you'll fit better. If you scoot underneath with a lantern, you can check for rotted boards."

Oliver groaned as his shoulders slumped. "Oh, very well. I hope there's nothing unfriendly under there." He went outside.

Irving followed. As he recalled, there was an open space beneath the back porch. Oliver could get under the house there. Oliver must have seen it too because once outside, that's where he was heading.

Sarah looked up from her work as they came into the backyard. "Is there something you need?"

Irving took in her ragged appearance. She was wearing the same ashen-gray dress as Saturday, an old apron, and once again, her hair was coming loose from its pins. Dark circles had formed under her eyes, and he wondered if she'd slept at all last night. "Do you need help?" he asked without thinking.

"No, I'm fine." She smiled weakly. "What is he doing?"

Irving turned to find Ollie crawling around the base of the back porch on his hands and knees. "Looking for the best way under the house. We want to make sure there arc no rotted boards other than in your bedroom. Do you have a lantern we could borrow?"

"Certainly." She wiped her hands on her apron and headed for the house.

Irving stayed with Oliver. She hadn't said much the

night he walked her and the children home. He thought maybe she was tired and even offered to let her ride Patch, but she refused.

After a moment, she returned holding a lantern. "Here you go."

Irving lit it, handed it to Oliver, then patted him on the back. "On your way now."

Ollie shuddered. "Snakes. Spiders. Maybe even a rat. Beasts of the dark. I hope you're happy I'm doing this for you."

Sarah giggled. "Are you always so dramatic?"

"He's nothing like Phileas," Irving said. "He's just being funny. Now get on with it, brother."

Oliver gave him a very dramatic roll of the eyes, then headed for the crawl space. He got on his belly and shimmied under the house, the lantern illuminating his way.

"Take a good look around," Irving called. "The bedroom is the worst. That's to your right."

"I see it," came the muffled reply.

"Is it safe under there?" Sarah asked with concern.

"I'm sure there's a few spiders, maybe even a rabbit, but nothing to …"

"Aaack!"

"Ollie?" Irving called. "Is everything all right?"

"No," was barely heard.

Irving approached the porch. "I say, what's the trouble?"

Oliver's booted feet appeared, then the rest of him as he scooted backward as fast as he could. He emerged with cobwebs in his hair and a smudge of dirt on his face. He was on his feet in an instant and backed away. "There's a family of funny looking cats under there! They stink. And I think they're feral."

Sarah looked puzzled for a moment. "Feral cats? But I've never seen any ... oh dear."

"What is it?" Irving asked.

She sighed. "Oliver, what color were these cats?"

"Black and white. They're the strangest looking things I've ever seen."

She put a hand over her mouth then snorted. "Oh, my word, those aren't cats. They're skunks!"

Sarah did her best not to laugh. "You're lucky you didn't get sprayed."

Irving and Oliver exchanged the same look of confusion. "Sprayed, you say?" Irving peered at the crawl space. "Sprayed with what?"

She crossed her arms and smiled. "You really don't want to find out."

"What were those things?" Oliver asked.

Her eyebrows shot up. "You don't have skunks in England?"

They shook their heads.

"Oh, I see." She peered at the crawl space. "I suspected one was hanging around, but I didn't think I had an entire family under my house." She rubbed her forehead with a hand. One more thing to worry about. Lovely. "I'm afraid you won't be able to crawl under the house without great risk. A skunk sprays anything they think is threatening it. Guaranteed, whatever *it* is won't threaten the skunk again anytime soon."

"Foul creatures, these skunks," Oliver said. "Yet so ... cute, in a way."

"Really?" Irving said. "How so?"

Oliver shrugged. "Fluffy tails, black with a wide white strip from the top of its little head to the tip of said tail, cute little nose ..."

Irving got down on his hands and knees and tried to see under the porch. "How can something so cute be so awful?"

"They're skunks," she said in explanation. "They stink to high heaven at times and can make you smell worse."

Irving climbed to his feet. "Well, so much for checking the floorboards beneath the house." He turned to her. "How do we get rid of them?"

"That's a good question," she said. "I've never had them under my house before." She heaved a sigh. "I wanted to get a dog for the children. It would have helped keep them away. But Caleb didn't want one. It was another mouth to feed."

"Dogs?" Oliver asked. "Do they chase them?"

"They help scare them off." She stared at the back porch. "Where were they, exactly?"

"I'd say between yours and the children's room."

"That explains the odd smell," Irving stated to no one in particular.

Sarah's cheeks heated. She was wondering if he'd catch the scent while working on her place, but as he hadn't said anything, she'd forgotten about the local wildlife. "The captain might know how to get rid of them."

"Ah, yes, the captain," Oliver said. "He's a right bright fellow. Perhaps Scampy could scare them off."

She made a face. "If that dog gets under the house and starts barking at those skunks, he'll get himself sprayed. It takes forever to get rid of the stench. Weeks if not longer."

"Oh, that doesn't sound pleasant," Irving said with a shudder. "No Scampy, then."

"But how do we get rid of them?" Oliver asked.

"Lure them out, I would think," Irving said. "What do they like to eat?"

She began to pace. "Bugs, maybe a few vegetables from the garden. They don't get into the garden like the rabbits do."

"Would the captain know?" Irving asked.

She rubbed the back of her neck. She could feel a headache coming on. "I'm sure he does, as would anyone else that's had this problem. I think the Atkinses had one living under their house once."

"We'll check with the captain." Irving studied her, and she blushed under his scrutiny. "You look tired."

She hugged herself and shrugged. "I'm fine." She let

her arms drop and headed for the washtub. "I have to finish my work."

He followed. "We'll check the rest of the floorboards, then help you."

Sarah turned to him. "No, that won't be necessary."

He looked into her eyes. "But we want to help."

She saw the sincerity in his eyes and part of her warmed. "I ... can manage."

He took a step closer. "If you're sure."

She swallowed and nodded. "Yes." She caught his scent, the same mix of cedar and roses, and realized it must come from the dresser in the hotel room where he kept his clothes. "I'll be fine."

"Very well," he said softly. "We'll take care of our business here, then pay a visit to the captain."

She swallowed again, her mouth dry. What was wrong with her? Her heart was beating like a humming-bird's and her belly was ... well, it was doing something, she couldn't say what. "Very good," she managed, then turned to the washtub. She was beginning to see what happened to Letty and Cassie.

The Darlings were all handsome men, and each with their own personality and mannerisms. Phileas was the most dramatic, bordering on flamboyant. He should be on the stage. Sterling was the obvious leader of the six. He was forthright, decisive, and at times, brooding. Oliver, she was learning, was more innocent, which made sense as he was the youngest. Conrad was, as she'd heard, the most outgoing – or as some referred to him, a flirt.

Wallis (she'd finally learned his correct name the other night) had a curious nature and asked a lot of questions about all kinds of things during their dinner.

And then there was Irving. He was calmer, quiet, and from what she'd observed so far, a thinker. So, what did he think of her now? She wasn't some rich farmer's widow. She was probably the most destitute person in Apple Blossom. She had nothing to offer the man for the work he was doing. She could barely offer him food.

The men finished what they could and prepared to leave. Oliver headed for the front gate while Irving lagged. "I wanted to ask you something," he said.

She stopped scrubbing. "Yes?"

"It's about Mrs. Winkle."

She smiled and turned around. "Oh?"

He smiled back. "I noticed Lacey is quite attached to her. And as anyone can see, poor Mrs. Winkle has seen better days."

Sarah nodded. "It's the eye. I'm surprised it hasn't fallen off yet. I'd best sew it on this evening."

"No, this isn't about her eye." He closed the distance between them and glanced around as if to make sure they were alone. "Would you mind if I purchased her a new doll?"

Her heart stopped. "I don't know what to say."

"I'll get Flint something too. I wouldn't want him to think I'm playing favorites."

She blinked a few times. "No, of course not. How generous of you."

He shrugged. "I just want her to enjoy something new. Flint too, for that matter. What does he like?"

She looked into his eyes. "Games."

He nodded. "Jolly good." He tipped his hat. "Until tomorrow."

She nodded again, unable to speak. She was suddenly mesmerized by him and couldn't understand why.

With a parting smile, Irving went to join his brother at the gate.

Sarah watched him go, her throat growing thick, and wondered if Letty or Cassie had battled with their heart the way she was beginning to battle with hers.

Chapter Seven

"Working on the Widow Crawford's house, are you?" Woodrow Atkins grabbed another piece of lumber off his buckboard, balanced it on his shoulder, then entered the feed store where he'd started another stack.

Conrad and Irving were helping him. "That's right," Irving said. "And I'm afraid the house needs a lot of work."

"What that house needs," Mr. Atkins said, "is to be torn down. But I suppose it could be a nice little place once it's fixed up. For someone. Mrs. Crawford, in my opinion, ought to move into town."

"Why?" Conrad asked. "Letty lives over a mile from town and has a ranch to take care of. She does fine by herself."

Mr. Atkins' gray eyebrows rose. "Letty doesn't have two young children to look after. That poor widow works herself to death and was doing it long before she lost her husband."

Irving exchanged a look of curiosity with his brother. "What do you mean?"

"Grab those boards there, boys," Mr. Atkins nodded at another stack in the buckboard. "As I was saying, Caleb was an all-right fella, just not very ambitious. He could have fixed things around that place a long time ago but was always riding off with Sheriff Laine, God rest his soul. Good man, but like Caleb, not very ambitious." He gave Conrad a pointed look. "As I'm sure you've discovered."

Conrad couldn't argue, so he nodded. "I haven't seen the widow's home yet, but if it's anything like Cassie's ..."

"It's worse," Irving cut in. "Much worse." He grabbed a couple of boards and carried them into the feed store.

Conrad followed. "Oliver hasn't said a word about it, and he's been out there with you."

"When has he had the chance?" Irving headed back to the wagon. "Has he told you about the skunks? I admit they slipped my mind."

"Skunks?" Mr. Atkins said. "Are you telling me Mrs. Crawford has skunks under her house?"

"A whole family," Irving said. "She educated Oliver and I about them. Nasty creatures all around. Oliver thought they were cute."

Conrad rolled his eyes. "He would. But what are they?"

"A nuisance," Mr. Atkins said. "I've been telling that woman to get a dog. They keep critters away."

"That's what she told Oliver and me," Irving said. "I don't think she can afford to keep one."

Mr. Atkins reached for another board. "I believe that." He nodded at the stack. "If you fellas don't mind grabbing those, I'd be much obliged." He turned and carried his load into the feed store.

"Is her place really that bad?" Conrad asked.

Irving sighed and nodded. "I was going to mention the floor last night, but we got on to the topic of you and Cassie. I'm glad you're happy, brother. Though I still can't get over you asking her to marry you."

Conrad grabbed another couple of boards. "Neither can I. Imagine me, a married man!"

"So, erm ... what are you going to do now?" Irving hedged. "You were tightlipped last night. Will you stay?"

"She *is* the sheriff," he pointed out.

"And you're her new deputy," Irving stated. "But that doesn't mean you have to stay. You could return to England, you know."

"I'm aware. However, I don't think Cassie will leave. This is her home, and she feels responsible for the people in this town." Conrad hefted a couple of boards onto his shoulder and headed inside.

Irving stared at the remaining two and sighed. If Sterling and Conrad stayed behind, Mother and Father would be furious. Well, he'd deal with it when the time came. He pushed the thought aside, grabbed the boards and followed Conrad.

In the feed store, the three men stood next to the stacked lumber. Mr. Atkins smiled. "Thanks, boys. That was mighty nice of you."

"Since we came to get lumber anyway," Irving said with a smile, "it all works out. I'll need a few pieces. Conrad?"

"Me too. Billy and I are building Cassie a new chicken coop."

Irving thought a moment. "I'll have to build Sarah one."

Conrad smiled. "Sarah? I know we agreed to be on a first-name basis the night she joined us for dinner, but I didn't think you'd do it."

Irving shrugged. "Why not? Everybody's on a first-name basis around here."

Mr. Atkins laughed. "That's true enough. Now if you don't mind, I'd best get back to my mill." He headed for his buckboard.

Irving looked at the stack of freshly cut lumber. "How much does one need for a chicken coop?"

Conrad smiled. "That depends on how big you want to make it."

Irving had seen Sarah's chicken coop briefly, and it wasn't very big. "I shan't need much."

Conrad nodded and returned outside. Irving followed. "Had we been smart," Conrad said. "We'd have chosen how much lumber we needed, then had Mr.

Atkins deliver it. First Cassie's and then Sarah's. Now we'll have to carry it, I'm afraid."

Irving made a show of looking up and down the street. "Where are Oliver and Wallis when you need them?" He laughed and returned to the lumber. He'd need at least half a dozen boards. "We'll have to borrow a wagon."

"Jean Campbell has one," Conrad said with a smile. "She's probably in the kitchen with Dora."

Irving looked at him, aghast. "The wagon she uses for funerals?"

"Try not to think about it." Conrad started off.

"Where are you going?" Irving asked and followed.

"To ask Jean about the wagon. We can take Cassie her lumber, take what you need to Sarah's, then I'll drive the wagon back, unhitch the horse and there you have it."

"Good man," Irving stated as they walked. "So, what do you make of Mr. Atkins' statements regarding the previous Sheriff Laine and Sarah's late husband?"

"Decent sorts, but not ones to rush to get a job done. I'd hate to think ill of either of them." Conrad gave him a sidelong glance. "Makes you wonder what some of the others in Apple Blossom are really like."

"So far, we only know a few of the women. Cassie, of course. Letty, Dora, and Jean." Irving cringed. "Oh, and Alma, but I'm in no hurry to get to know her well."

Conrad laughed. "That makes two of us. And Sarah?"

Irving turned his head toward Sarah's place. "She doesn't trust me." He looked at Conrad. "Not a whit. Normally, I wouldn't be bothered, but for some reason I am."

"I know the feeling, brother." Conrad clasped his hands behind his back as they strolled toward the hotel. "Cassie didn't trust me either. But perhaps for different reasons."

Irving made a face. "You flirted with her, didn't you?"

"Can I help it if I'm friendly?" he teased. "But seriously, I didn't at first. I think it started with that fishing trip with Billy."

"You'll have to show me his fishing hole," Irving said. "Might be fun to go."

Conrad gave him a playful shove. "Best not take Sarah. You might fall in love." He waggled his eyebrows and entered the hotel.

Jean was in the kitchen with Dora baking cookies. "Irving, Conrad," Dora said. "What are you two doing here?"

"I thought both of you were working," Jean added.

"And so we are." Conrad plucked a cookie off a plate.

Irving looked over the pile. "I say, I've never eaten so many cookies before. Plenty of biscuits mind you, but not cookies." He grabbed one and took a generous bite.

Dora laughed. "Would you like some tea to go with them? A sandwich?"

"Jean's wagon." Irving took another bite. "We need

to transfer some lumber to Cassie's house and then Sarah's. Do you mind?"

"Well, no," Jean said. "But you'll have to hitch up my horse. You do know which one is mine, don't you?"

Conrad nodded. "The speckled-gray gelding, correct?"

"Mr. Brown, I believe?" Irving smiled at her. "I don't think I've ever met a horse with a surname."

"I told Pa he should have named him Mr. Gray but no, he liked Mr. Brown." Jean grabbed a cookie off a sheet and took a bite.

"Is there anything else you need while you're here?" Dora asked. "Are you sure you're not hungry?"

"Gad, woman," Conrad said. "I feel for the man that marries you. He'll weigh as much as an elephant before your first anniversary."

Dora grabbed a dishtowel and snapped it at him. "Stop that. He'll be fit as a fiddle."

Conrad grimaced and rubbed his arm. "Regardless, he should be warned. You're always trying to feed us."

"I wouldn't mind a couple of sandwiches," Irving said. "And a few cookies."

"That's right, you're working out of town." Dora went to the hutch, pulled out a small sack and began to fill it with cookies. "I'll make four sandwiches, one for each of you." With a knowing smile she set the sack aside.

Irving smiled warmly in return. "Thank you, Dora. You are most kind."

"Sarah's proud, you know." Dora headed for the larder.

"I'm beginning to see that." He turned to Conrad. "What about Cassie?"

His brother shook his head. "Proud, yes, but from the sounds of it, not so much as Sarah."

"I feel for her," Irving said. "She can barely feed herself and those children. Who knows what will become of them this winter?"

Dora returned with ingredients for sandwiches. "Why don't you two hitch up the wagon while I make these?"

"Jolly good idea," Irving said. "Conrad?"

"Right behind you, brother."

They went to the livery stable and fetched Mr. Brown. As soon as they had him hitched to Jean's wagon, they picked up Irving's lunch and a few extra cookies for Conrad, then went to gather their lumber.

Irving, bringing lunch, wondered if Sarah would accept it. But why wouldn't she? It was just a few sandwiches and cookies. She wasn't that proud, was she? He supposed he'd soon find out.

Sarah finished her first basket of laundry and started rinsing. This was the hard part for her, wringing out the clothes. Her rinse water was lukewarm at this point. By the time she was done with the second load, it would be cold.

Once again, she thought about winter and the freezing temperatures. Maybe she should consider moving to town and finding a bigger space. But how could she afford one? Even if her place sold, would she get a decent price? There were so many "what ifs" that it made her head swim just thinking about them.

A sound caught her attention. Was that a wagon? She wiped her hands on her apron and headed for the front of the house. Sure enough, one came into view as she reached the front yard. Her heart skipped a beat. "Irving, Conrad." She headed for the gate. "That looks like Jean's wagon."

"It is." Irving climbed down. "She let us borrow it so we could bring some lumber out. I've decided to build you a new chicken coop."

She gasped in delight. "Irving, you are too kind." Tears stung her eyes, and she blinked them away. She would not let the man see her cry. "Thank you so much."

"It's our pleasure," Conrad said. "Irving, the sack?"

"Oh, yes." He went to the front of the wagon and took a sack from beneath the seat. "Dora sent lunch. Wasn't that nice of her?"

Sarah swallowed hard. She hadn't thought about what she was going to do for lunch. She'd run out of bread and didn't have a chance to bake any this morning. "How nice. I'll thank her the next time I get to town."

Irving went through the gate and headed up the

walk. "I'll put this in the kitchen. It's sandwiches and cookies."

Flint came running out of the house. "Did I hear cookies?"

Irving held the sack up high over his head. "You did. And you don't get any until after you've eaten your sandwich. Is that understood?"

"Ah, gee whiz. Can't a hard-working man get a cookie when he needs one?"

Everyone laughed. "I do hope you get your share, brother," Conrad said. "Put that in the house and let's get this lumber unloaded."

"You heard the man," Irving said. "Let's put this in the kitchen. Then you can help us unload."

Flint grinned and ran into the house.

Sarah joined Irving on the front porch. "That boy. Last night he talked about getting a pipe like the captain's."

"Oh, dear," Irving groaned. "He's a little young for that."

"Indeed. But he likes to emulate the captain. As do a lot of the children."

"They think highly of him, don't they?" Irving said.

She nodded. "They do. And so long as he doesn't take them on some wild goose chase after his elusive sea beast, no one minds him teaching the children their reading, writing and arithmetic. He's quite smart that way."

Irving motioned her inside. "Is he, now? I've yet to have a conversation with him. Conrad, on the other hand, has spent time with him. Nice chap, he says." In the kitchen, he gave her the sack of food and returned to the wagon.

She took out the contents of the sack, then fetched some plates from the hutch. As it was nearly lunchtime, they might as well eat. What a blessing to have what she needed when she needed it. Still, she didn't want to have to rely on charity and reminded herself to bake bread first thing in the morning before starting her laundry.

"Mama?" Lacey said as she entered the kitchen.

"Yes, sweetheart?"

"What's Mr. Darling doing with the other Mr. Darling outside?"

"They've brought lumber for the house and to build a new chicken coop. Would you like some lunch?" She looked at the food Irving brought and sighed. "Dora made cookies and sandwiches for us. Wasn't that nice?"

Lacey approached the worktable. "Why didn't you make us lunch?"

An icy feeling settled in the pit of her stomach. "Because I've been busy working. I forgot we needed bread and didn't make any this morning."

Lacey looked at the sandwiches. "They look good. Can I have one now?"

"Of course. Sit down." Sarah put a sandwich on a plate and brought it to the table. "Let me get you something to drink."

Lacey didn't say anything and instead stared at the food. The sandwiches were large – she doubted Lacey could finish one. Flint might be able to. Outside she filled a pitcher with water, brought it into the kitchen and filled four glasses.

It wasn't long before Irving and Flint joined them. "Look how big those sandwiches are," Flint commented with wide eyes.

She pulled out a chair for him. "Sit down and you can have yours."

Flint took a seat and licked his lips.

Irving laughed as he sat next to him. "Hungry?"

"I'm starved," Flint said. "Dora makes good sandwiches. She's a good cook."

"That she is." Irving patted his stomach. "I'm surprised I haven't gained twenty pounds."

"You're working hard," Sarah commented. "Thank you." The dread in her gut sank a little lower. She'd have to come up with a solution to winter sooner than later. "Let us pray."

Everyone clasped their hands and bowed their heads. Sarah did the same as weariness washed over her. "Dear Lord, bless this food and the hands that prepared it. Bless Irving for helping with the house and bless Flint for helping him."

"What about me?" Lacey blurted.

Sarah looked at her. "Wait until after the blessing is done, young lady."

Lacey frowned and closed her eyes again.

Sarah continued. "Thank you for all the work the Darlings are doing for the people in this town. Amen."

Lacey's eyes popped open. "Mama, you still didn't say anything about me."

"Are you helping Mr. Darling with the house?"

Lacey looked at everyone, then at Mrs. Winkle. "Well, no."

Sarah sighed. "I can't thank you for something you haven't done, sweetheart. Maybe you can help with another job when it starts."

"Painting, perhaps?" Irving put a napkin on his lap. "How does that sound?"

Lacey giggled.

Flint looked at him, horrified. "You don't know what you're saying."

"I'm saying she can paint." He looked at Sarah. "That's a good thing, right?"

Sarah slowly shook her head. "Not really."

Lacey cackled as she reached for her sandwich.

Irving's eyebrows shot up in alarm. "I say, was that a maniacal giggle? Or did she always sound like that?"

"What does man-i-a-cal mean?" Flint picked up his sandwich and looked it over, deciding where to bite into it first.

Irving let loose a maniacal laugh to demonstrate, making the children jump. "There, that's what it means."

Flint and Lacey took one look at each other and flew into hysterics.

Sarah shook her head. "Now see what you've done! We'll be lucky to make it through lunch."

He laughed softly. "All part of my evil plan, my dear."

She blushed at his playfulness and, for a moment, forgot about the coming winter and all the misery it would bring. "You're a silly man at times, Irving Darling."

"It's nice to be silly now and then." He picked up his sandwich. "*Bon appétit.*" He took a generous bite and chewed.

Sarah began eating and watched the others. The children liked Irving, and she had to admit she was beginning to like him too. Perhaps too much. He was kind, generous, and had the most wondrous blue eyes she'd ever seen. If she were smart, she'd stop thinking about those eyes along with the rest of him. He was a distraction she couldn't afford.

She took a few more bites of her sandwich, then wrapped it in a napkin.

"What are you doing?" Irving asked.

"Could you sit with the children while they finish their lunch?" She carried the sandwich to the worktable and set it down. "I need to get back to my laundry."

"Must you?" He got to his feet.

"I'm afraid I've dallied too long as it is. If you'll excuse me." She headed for the back door.

Irving hurried to her side. "Sarah, are you truly not hungry?"

Unfortunately for her, her belly decided to growl. She looked at it, then him. "I'm fine."

He sighed and shook his head. "I dare say you're not.

At least finish half, save the rest for later. How can you work if you don't have your strength?"

He had a point. "Well." She went to the worktable, unwrapped her sandwich and took a bite.

He shook his head again, took her by the shoulders and steered her back to the kitchen table. "Sit, rest, eat. It's how you get work done."

"What?" She looked at her sandwich, then him.

He put his hands on his hips and stared down at her like a schoolmaster. "If you don't take care of yourself, dear woman, how are you going to take care of them?" He looked at Flint and Lacey.

A chill went up Sarah's spine. He was right. She closed her eyes a moment, nodded, then took another bite of her sandwich.

Chapter Eight

Irving watched Sarah nibble at her food. There was a fear in her eyes, an unrest that looked as if no matter how much sleep she got, she would still be tired. Her days were full of toil, and he thought of his father's tenants back home. None of them lived like this. His father saw to that and taught his sons to do the same. It was one of the reasons he made them work on their tenants' homes repairing roofs, porches, fencing, barns and outbuildings. They earned their tenants' respect and learned to appreciate the people that worked their family's lands.

She finished her sandwich and took her empty plate to the dry sink. "Children, are you done?"

"I can't eat mine," Lacey said. "It's too big."

Sarah came to the table and took her plate. "Then you can have the rest for dinner." She looked at her son. "Flint?"

The boy shoved his plate toward her. "Save mine too."

Irving noted Flint ate only half as well. Was that why Sarah only wanted half of hers? Were they counting on the rest to be their dinner? Oh bother, had he just deprived Sarah of her next meal? His heart ached at the thought and something inside him stirred. "I thought we could have dinner together."

Flint's eyes widened, and he whispered something to Lacey.

She ignored them, looked at Irving, then stared at the table. "No, that's not …"

"I'll stop by Alma's and pick up a few things. We can discuss paint and what to do in the children's bedroom." He smiled at her then took another bite of his sandwich.

Sarah stared at him in fear and anticipation. She didn't know what to do with the offer. "I …"

"You don't have to worry about a thing," he assured, putting his hand over hers.

She looked at their hands. "Irving … you're too kind."

"I try. We all do." He patted her hand. "It doesn't hurt to let us."

She drew her hand back and gripped Flint's plate. "Of course not. We're all appreciative of what you and your brothers have done for us."

He gave her a warm smile. If Father's tenants were all like Sarah Crawford, what would he do? How would he help them? He might consider this practice. After all, he'd have to deal with a lot of people daily if he had to take over the title and estate. He just wished there weren't so many unknowns. Who knew if Sterling would stay? Who knew how long Father would live? And who knew how much he could learn from him beforehand? He hated being unprepared – it scared him. Because Heaven forbid, he fail ...

"I should wrap Flint's sandwich, then get back to work." Sarah went to the worktable.

Irving watched her then nudged Flint with his elbow. "How about you? Are you ready to get to work?"

"Yes, sir!" Flint pushed his chair from the table, headed for the back door and stopped. "Mr. Darling, what are we doing?"

"We're going to tear apart the fence." He grinned. "Won't that be fun?"

Flint smiled. "Yeah!" He ran out the door.

Sarah shook her head. "Why do boys love to tear things apart?"

Irving smiled. "We just do." He left the table and went to the door. "We'll be in the front if you need us and probably head to town later. I'll need to see if Mr. Atkins has any fencing at the feed store. I forgot to check when Conrad and I were there earlier ..." He looked into her eyes, saw the weariness in them, and fought the urge to pull her into his arms. By Jove, she was irresistible. So fragile, so ... oh bother, she looked like she needed to be held. Badly. He swallowed hard and turned to the door.

"Fine, Lacey and I will be in the back." Sarah wrapped Flint's sandwich in a napkin.

Irving gave her one last look and went outside. As soon as he stepped off the porch, he took a deep breath. He couldn't afford to get close to this woman. It would only end in heartbreak, and he didn't want to do that to her or the children. He was having a moment of deep compassion, that's all. He'd do the same for his father's tenants.

He went to the front of the house where Flint was waiting. "What do we do first?" the boy asked.

"Well," Irving looked the fence over and rubbed his face. His heart was still with Sarah, watching her, reaching for her ...

"Mr. Darling?"

"Right, the fence." He stepped to the gate, went through, and began to examine the fence and posts. "This one," he said when he reached the third post down the line. "This needs to be replaced." He motioned Flint to join him. "See this?" He took out his room key from the hotel and poked at the wood. "See how easy I can jab my key into the post?"

"Uh-huh."

Irving's eyes went to the house, and he had to force himself to look at Flint. "That means the wood is rotting. We'll use the hammer to pull the fence away from the post, salvage what fencing is still good, then replace the post and whatever fencing has to be tossed."

"That sounds like a lot of work." Flint crossed his arms. "I think I should be paid a fair wage for my labor."

Irving blinked a few times, then laughed. "You've been talking to Billy."

Flint grinned. "He told me a worker is worth his wages. It's in the Good Book, you know."

"So it is. Well then, young man, what do you propose I do about it?"

Flint's face screwed up. "Pay me?"

Irving smiled. He liked teasing him. "Fine. I'll see that you're paid for your, um, labors." He looked the boy over. "Let's see, you can haul lumber for me like a pack horse."

Flint's eyes almost popped from his head. "What?!"

Irving laughed, harder this time. "On second thought, you'll work up such an appetite, there won't be enough food in Apple Blossom to feed you."

Flint frowned. "There isn't now."

Irving's amusement faded. "How is that?"

Flint stuck his hands in his pockets. "Ah, it's nothing."

Irving got down on one knee and looked at the child. "Flint, are you not getting enough to eat?"

He shrugged, his face turning redder by the second. "I shouldn't have said anything."

Irving took him by the shoulders. "It's all right, Flint. But if you, your mother and sister don't have enough to eat, I'd like to know."

His face went redder still. "Ma don't like it when people think we're poor."

Irving smiled. "I understand."

"But ..." Flint hung his head. "Sometimes I'm still hungry after we've eaten supper, and there's no more food." He looked at Irving. "It's not that we ain't got food, Mr. Darling. Just not enough of it. That's why I like it when we have dinner with the captain. We should all have dinner with him tonight." He gave him a hopeful look.

He nodded. "I see. Thank you for sharing that with me. As to the captain, perhaps some other time."

Flint grabbed hold of his arm. "Don't tell Ma what I said."

Irving met the boy's eyes. "I won't say a word." He gave Flint a quick hug, then released him. "We'd better get back to work. We still need to go to town for more supplies."

"We're going to Alma's?"

"I just said so, didn't I?" He took the hammer to the post and in one swift move, pulled a section of fencing from it.

Flint's eyes widened. "You sure are strong, Mr. Darling."

He smiled and pulled more fencing down. There were entire sections that needed to be replaced. This chore alone could take a couple of days, but he'd see it done.

They worked for the next hour and removed not

only the bad fencing, but all the rotted posts. "There, now that that's done, let's take a walk to town."

Flint wiped his brow with his shirt and looked over what they'd accomplished. "That's a lot of fence. Billy won't believe I helped take that down."

"I'll vouch for you." Irving looked at the house. "Why don't you tell your mother we're leaving?"

"Okay." Flint ran around the house to the back. Irving stood and waited for his return. He didn't want to speak with Sarah now. It was bad enough he'd been thinking about her while he and Flint tore the fence apart. The little family didn't get enough to eat, and it bothered him to his core. He wanted to help but wasn't sure how. Sure, he could give them funds for food, but what about after he and his brothers were gone? Then what would they do? Anything he gave them would run out eventually and that would be that.

No, Sarah needed something sustainable to get them through the coming winter and keep plenty of food on the table. Flint was what, six? If he was hungry now, what about when he was older?

Lacey ran around the corner of the house clutching Mrs. Winkle. "Can I go too?"

He looked at her, hands on hips. "Can you walk that far?"

She nodded. "Me and Mrs. Winkle both can. We walk to town all the time."

Irving smiled warmly. "That's right, you do." He

rubbed his chin a few times. "Well, so long as it's all right with your mother."

"Oh, it is!" She spun on her little heel and ran for the back of the house. "Mama? Can I go to town with Mr. Darling?"

Irving laughed and shook his head. "Children." He put his hand over his heart. It was ... warming. "Children indeed."

Sarah came around the house. "Lacey is going on about accompanying you to town. Is she putting words in your mouth?"

He took in the sight of her, wet apron and all. She was beautiful. He looked upward, pretending to examine the roof. "Not at all. She can come if she wants."

"I don't want her to be a nuisance."

He smiled, drew in a breath, then looked at her. "She won't be."

"Well." Sarah wiped her hands on her apron. "Then I suppose it's all right."

Lacey tiptoed to stand behind her mother. "Boo!"

Sarah jumped, her hand to her chest. "Oh, my! How do you sneak up on me like that?" She turned to the child and hugged her.

Lacey laughed. "I tell Mrs. Winkle to be real quiet."

Sarah released her. "What a good job Mrs. Winkle did. Now tell her to behave herself while you walk to town. Be good in Alma's store."

"I will." Lacey ran to Irving. "Let's go!"

He looked beyond Sarah. "Where's Flint?"

"In the privy," Lacey said. "That means we can get a head start."

"They race each other to town," Sarah explained.

Irving smiled, took another breath, and waited for Flint. The sooner they headed to town, the better – if only so he wouldn't be staring at Sarah.

Sarah returned to work and hadn't been scrubbing long when Irving came by. "Is something wrong?" she asked. She looked past him but didn't see the children.

"The children insist you go with us."

She shook her head. "Oh, no, I ..."

He held up a hand. "I'll help you upon our return."

She stared at him. "What?"

"Promise." He smiled. "The children really want you to go."

Her shoulders slumped. "Oh, dear."

"I can scrub and rinse if you like," he offered.

"It's not that." She finished scrubbing the pants she was working on. "I don't want the children to think I can just up and leave my work."

"Then they'll help too. It's all give and take, really." He smiled again.

Her shoulders slumped some more. Did she have the energy to walk to town and back? "Very well." She wiped her hands on her already-wet apron, then took it off. "But just this once."

"Of course." He offered his arm. "Shall we?"

She stared at it, her heart suddenly pounding. Merciful heavens, he was only being a gentleman. Sarah blinked a few times as tears stung her eyes. Yes, he was a gentleman, but she was learning that he was so much more. Irving Darling was a kind, hardworking man. He was good with the children, had patience, and tried to do his best by them. In short, he was the kind of man a woman hoped to marry ...

"Something wrong?" he asked softly.

Her heart melted on the spot. "I ... I was trying to think of anything I need."

"Think on the way." He offered his arm again.

She took it, felt his bicep through his shirt, and her heart skipped a beat. Oh, goodness! She couldn't afford to get attached! For one, he was leaving. She thought of pulling her arm from his, but that would be rude.

"Mama!" Lacey cried when they reached the front of the house. "You came!" She grinned at Flint.

"Yes, sweetheart. But only because all of you are going to help me finish my laundry when we get back."

Flint grimaced. "Yuck. Wet clothes to wring out."

"That's my job," Irving said. "You two can take the dry clothes off the line, fold them, then take them into the house for your mother."

"Oh," Flint said. "That's not so bad." He turned to her. "No offense, Ma, but ain't laundry women's work?"

She sighed. "It's work I get paid for."

"Oh," he said again and hung his head. "Sorry."

"Can I get paid to work?" Lacey asked.

"Sure," Irving said. "But we have to find something you can do well." He glanced at the downed fencing. "And I have just the job in mind." He looked at Sarah and smiled.

"Whitewashing?" she mouthed.

He nodded. "All right, children, let's get to town." They filed through the gate, which made her smile considering half the fence was down.

Once on the road, Flint and Lacey raced ahead as usual, then started skipping. She smiled at the sight. If she hadn't a care in the world, she'd be skipping too. But that wasn't the case.

"They're happy children," Irving commented.

She noticed he still had her arm looped around his. She extracted herself, went to the other side of the road and picked a daisy. "Yes." She rejoined him but didn't take his arm. It wouldn't do to walk arm in arm all the way to town. "Lacey, come here."

Lacey turned and ran to them. "What, Mama?"

Sarah put the daisy in her hair. "There now, isn't that pretty?"

Lacey touched it, smiled, then ran to catch up with Flint.

Irving smiled at her. "She's a lovely child. They both are." He winked. "But don't let Flint know I said that. He's in a hurry to become a man."

"I know. He's been that way ever since Caleb passed."

She looked at the dusty road as they walked. "The world asks too much of children at times."

"Too much of you?"

She smiled weakly. "That too."

"You're tired," he stated. "You need rest."

She wanted to laugh but kept her mouth shut. She forced a smile instead. "I do what I have to."

He stopped and turned to her. "Sarah, let me help you."

Her heart stopped. "What?"

"There's got to be something you can do other than toil over a washtub all day. The work is backbreaking, and you make next to nothing."

She gaped at him. "It's ... it's none of your business, you know."

"I do. I'm choosing to make it my business. At least check into some things."

"What things? There's nothing, Irving, nothing I can do but take in laundry. I have no special skills."

"I hear you're a good seamstress. What about the empty millinery shop?"

Her hands went to her hips. "There's no guarantee I'd get any business. Besides, I'd have to sell my place, and who knows if it would sell. If by some miracle it does, what I get for it might not be enough to purchase the millinery and its living quarters. The bank took it over after Mrs. O'Halloran left."

"Then we'll speak to Mr. Featherstone." He gently

took her arms. "You won't know until you ask. Isn't it worth a try?"

She sighed and tried to ignore the warmth of his large hands through the fabric of her sleeves. "I don't see the point."

"Don't? How about won't? You're scared."

She backed away. "Yes, I am. And if you were in my position, you would be too."

He sighed and looked to the sky. Was he sending up a prayer? "I apologize. I didn't mean to speak out of turn."

She hugged herself. "I suppose not. But it really is none of your business."

He closed the distance between them and glanced up the road. "I still want to help."

She followed his gaze. Flint and Lacey had skipped about fifty yards ahead. "Finish your work on the house, then be free of us."

He frowned. "Free of you? As if you're a burden to me?" He stepped away, took off his hat and ran his hand through his thick dark hair. "My dear woman, I am doing this because I want to, not because I must. I'm not duty bound to help you – none of us are. We see a need and are trying to fill it." He put on his hat, went to her and put his hands on her shoulders. "We're simply being kind."

Her entire body warmed as the heat of his hands crept into her shoulders and beyond. She missed being held by a man, even if Caleb wasn't the most affectionate.

He at least hugged her now and then. She closed her eyes. "I'm sorry I snapped at you."

He gave his vest, or waistcoat as he liked to call it, a tug. "Very good then, no harm done." He looked at the road. "We'd best catch up to Flint and Lacey."

"Yes." She took a breath after he removed his hands and started off. She could grow more than attached to this man. The sooner he finished working on her house the better off she'd be. But what he said made sense. And unfortunately, he was right; she *was* scared. What if things didn't work out? If she sold her place but couldn't get into something else, they'd have no roof over their heads and would be worse off than they already were. She shuddered at the thought and followed Irving.

He waited for her to catch up, then walked beside her in silence. Was he giving her time to think about things?

She tried to think of supplies they needed instead, then rolled her eyes. She'd forgotten to bring money along. It figured. They could use some sugar and a few other odds and ends but would have to fetch them tomorrow when she delivered the laundry. That is, if she had enough money. Mrs. Featherstone only paid half of what she owed for the last delivery, claiming Mr. Featherstone's shirts weren't ironed properly and that she'd have to re-iron the lot. If that kept up, she'd have to find an extra customer to make up the difference and there was no one else in Apple Blossom that wanted their washing done.

Sarah pushed the thought aside and concentrated on

putting one foot in front of the other. Maybe Irving was right, she had to at least try. It was a risk, yes, but how else would she know? Did she really want to keep doing this the rest of her days? Would Lacey end up being nothing more than a washerwoman herself? The thought made her cringe. She would see Lacey married and well.

She glanced at Irving and sent up a prayer that the good Lord would bring her a man like him.

Chapter Nine

I rving watched Sarah out of the corner of one eye. He didn't want to say more as he didn't want to offend her. Her fear was holding her back, and he would have her fight it if he could. The question was how? He never experienced paralyzing fear himself. True, the thought of taking over the estate and title were daunting, but it wasn't something he couldn't handle in the long run. It meant a lot of work, a lot of time, and no small amount of headache. And his mother would drive him positively mad.

What Sarah suffered was much worse. She was afraid to move forward, even if it meant having a better life for herself and her children. But the unknown was always scary, and he had to figure out a way to convince her to step into it. He would be there at her side, but so far, she didn't believe him.

He supposed he couldn't blame her. They would be

leaving in a week or two. If they stayed longer, it would be because Phileas was digging his heels in over the hotel. He'd want everything perfect before he left. As long as everyone was okay with it and they made it to San Francisco on time, it was no problem.

As they entered the general store, Alma gave them a wide smile. "Sarah, Lacey, Flint," she said happily. "Good afternoon." She caught sight of Irving, and her smile grew. "Mr. Darling, how nice to see you again." She came around the counter. "Have you heard the news?"

"Dare we ask?" Irving said. Though he could guess.

"I *know* you've heard it, Mr. Darling," she gushed. "After all, Conrad is your brother."

He went to the counter and leaned against it. "If you're referring to my brother's recent declaration of love for the sheriff, then dear me, I haven't heard a thing."

Alma laughed. "You're so silly. But yes, that's it! Isn't it exciting? My goodness! What will Cassie do?"

Irving sighed. "I haven't the foggiest." He winked at Sarah.

Alma was on him like glue. "Is your brother going to stay? Is Cassie going to leave? Everyone is talking about it and wants to know."

"And last week everyone was talking about Sterling and Letty. Have they forgotten about them so soon?"

"Of course not," she said. "But we can only handle so much gossip at once and the six of you have ... well, brought a lot to town." She grinned then went behind the counter. "What do you need, Sarah?"

"Not me." Sarah pointed over her shoulder. "Him."

Irving approached the counter. "I'm going to need some fence posts, not to mention fencing for a picket fence. I understand Mr. Atkins has some precut?"

"Yes, at the feed store. But what can I get you?"

"Sorry, I was thinking aloud. I'll need some white-wash, more nails, an extra hammer ..."

Flint's eyes lit up. "Really?"

Irving nodded. "I think your hammering skills are good enough to warrant your own tool. So long as you're careful."

"I will be!" Flint said excitedly.

"Do I get a tool?" Lacey asked.

Irving bent to her. "Hmmm, let me think. Perhaps what you need is a helper. Or at least Mrs. Winkle does."

Lacey looked at her doll and sighed. "It's true. Mrs. Winkle can't get around the way she used to."

"I dare say you're right." He took Lacey by the hand and led her to the end of the counter. "Alma, do you have anyone here who could assist Mrs. Winkle with her work?"

Alma smiled. "Oh, right. Let's see." She went to a shelf at the other end of the counter and removed several rectangular boxes. She brought all three and set them down. "Lacey, let's introduce Mrs. Winkle to three possible helpers. Then she can decide who it will be."

Lacey gave them a wide-eyed look, then glanced at her mother. "Mama?"

Sarah shook her head. "Irving ..."

He held up a hand then nodded at the boxes. "It's perfectly fine. Mrs. Winkle?"

Lacey held up Mrs. Winkle as if she could examine the boxes.

Alma took the lid off one and presented it to Lacey. Inside was a beautiful dark-haired china doll wearing a blue dress. The doll had bright blue eyes and was a pretty thing. "Well, Mrs. Winkle," Alma said. "What do you think?"

Lacey didn't speak at first, instead staring at the doll.

"I believe Mrs. Winkle is thinking it over," Irving said. "Who's the next candidate?"

Alma opened the second box. It contained another china doll. This one had blonde hair, blue eyes, and wore a pink dress. It was just as beautiful and delicate as the first.

Lacey gasped as she stared at it.

"And the third candidate?" Irving asked.

The next box wasn't as fancy as the first two. In fact, it was a simple brown box and smaller. Alma took off the lid. Inside was a rag doll with two long braids made from yellow yarn. Its eyes were brown and embroidered into the fabric, as were its nose and mouth. Her cheeks were slightly pink, her hands like mittens. The doll's dress was blue and trimmed in white lace. She wore a white apron over it that was tied into a big bow in the back.

Lacey gawked at it like it was a pot of gold.

Irving got down on one knee. "Now, of the three

candidates, which one do you think Mrs. Winkle would get along with best?"

Lacey looked at the two fancy china dolls, then the rag doll, and pointed at the latter. "Mrs. Winkle likes that one." She turned to him, her little face serious. "She says they might be related."

"Oh?" Irving replied with raised eyebrows. "Is that so? Distant relation, eh?" He looked at Mrs. Winkle. "Madam, shall I escort your relative home? I'm sure she'll be able to help you with a number of tasks around the house."

Lacey continued to stare wide-eyed at the new doll. "She's so pretty."

Irving got to his feet. "Indeed, she is, young lady. You'll take good care of her, won't you?"

Lacey looked at him in awe. "I will. I promise!"

Sarah approached. "You're very kind. Thank you." She turned away, and he caught her wiping a tear from her eye. It warmed him to his toes.

"Flint, why don't you go to the back and pick out your new hammer?" Irving waved in that direction.

Flint grinned and ran for the back of the store.

"Walk, please!" Sarah called after him. "And don't pick the biggest one." She looked at Irving. "You know he will."

"Perhaps you'd best make sure he doesn't bring back a sledgehammer."

She smiled and followed her son.

"That was very nice of you," Alma said. "Poor Mrs.

Winkle is about to fall apart for the last time. I notice her eye is gone."

"By Jove, you're right. Poor thing."

"Mrs. Winkle or Lacey?" Alma said with a laugh. "But really, Mr. Darling. I know Sarah appreciates what you're doing."

"I don't know about that. I mentioned buying Lacey a doll a few days ago yet she balked. Well, never mind that. Wrap the doll up, will you? I'll ask Sarah what else she needs. We might as well get it while we're here."

"What about the fencing and posts?" Alma asked. "How are you going to get everything back to Sarah's place?"

"I'll borrow Jean's horse and wagon again." He felt a tug on his pants leg. It was Lacey. "Yes, my dear?"

"May I hold Mrs. Winkle's relation?"

He smiled at Alma. "I don't see why not. We'll bring her box, shall we? It would make a lovely bed for her."

Alma took the doll out of the box and handed it to Lacey. "What are you going to call her?"

"She already has a name. Mrs. Winkle will tell me what it is."

Alma smiled and exchanged a look of delight with Irving. It warmed his heart to see Lacey happy, and he wanted to see the same look on Flint's face. Even if he was just getting a hammer. To each his own.

"Alma, while I'm here, I'd like to get a few other things. As I'm borrowing Jean's wagon, then why don't you give me twenty pounds of flour, six pounds of coffee, ten pounds of sugar, a pound of carrots, three pounds of potatoes ..." He continued to rattle off a list including tooth powder, some toiletries for Sarah, a checkerboard for the children, a dozen skeins of yarn in various colors, and a few other things he knew would help the little family. "There, that ought to do it. We'll fetch Jean's wagon while you're putting that together."

Alma's lower lip trembled, and she covered her mouth.

"Whatever is the matter?" he asked.

She shook her head. "It's just that ... you're so kind. And she needs so much." She shook her head again and retreated behind the counter to fill his order.

He watched Sarah and Flint come his way, the latter admiring a shiny new hammer. Kindness could go a long way, so long as it was accepted. He hoped and prayed Sarah wouldn't reject his when they returned to fetch the supplies he was purchasing.

"Shall we go to the feed store?" he asked.

"But the children's things," Sarah said. "Shouldn't we ... I mean ..."

"I'm getting a few other things and will take care of the children's when we return." He smiled warmly and motioned her toward the door.

"Yes, of course," she said. "Come on, children." She ushered them to the door, Lacey clutching her new doll and Mrs. Winkle close to her chest.

Irving winked once more at Alma, then followed.

They crossed the street to the hotel, found only Dora

in the kitchen, then, after Lacey showed off her new doll, went to the undertaker's. Jean was in the back with a stack of lumber. "What are you doing?" Irving asked.

"Wallis offered to help me," she said. "He should be here any minute."

Irving lookcd at the unusual cut of the pieces. "You're going to build ..."

Jean glanced at the children and back. "Well, I am the undertaker in town."

"Indeed you are. Well, then, you and Wallis have fun. By the way, can we borrow your wagon again?"

Sarah appreciated Irving and Jean's veiled conversation in front of the children. They didn't need to know that Jean and Wallis would be building coffins.

They went to the livery, fetched Jean's horse, hitched it to the wagon, then went next door to the feed store. Flint made a show of helping Irving load the posts and fencing, then tried to stick his hammer in his back pocket, but it wouldn't fit. Next, he tried hanging it off his belt loop but that didn't work either. So, he held it, giving the tool admiring looks as he sat proudly on the wagon seat next to Irving.

Lacey sat in the back with her dolls, and Sarah walked along the boardwalk back to Alma's, watching them. They looked so happy her heart threatened to break. The children were getting attached to Irving, something she couldn't afford. They'd already lost their father; they didn't need to lose a father figure to boot. She shouldn't have let him purchase things for Flint and Lacey. She remembered him mentioning doing so but didn't think he'd come through. She couldn't deny them their gifts at this point, but she'd have to make sure he didn't do it again.

By the time they returned to the store, Alma had a huge pile of wrapped packages stacked on the counter next to big bags of flour, sugar, and what was probably coffee. "My goodness," Sarah said as she glanced around the store. "Whose order is that?"

Alma nodded at Irving. "His."

Sarah's jaw dropped. "What?" She spun to him. "What do you need all this for?"

"Well, as working men ..." He pulled Flint next to him. "... we require sustenance on a daily basis. I'm making sure you can provide it to us."

She stared at the pile of goods. "Ir ... Irving, please ..."

He let Flint go and went to her. "Sarah, the children need food. So do you."

She shook her head. "It's too much."

"It's simply what's needed." He patted her shoulder, then turned to Alma. "Care to help us?"

"Certainly." Alma took a few packages and came around the counter. "Flint, Lacey, grab some and follow me."

They did as she said, taking what packages they could carry and heading out the door after her.

Sarah and Irving were now quite alone. She looked at him. "You shouldn't have."

"Yes, I should. I had to."

Sarah shook her head. "You don't know what you're doing."

"On the contrary." He closed the distance between them. "I'm doing what my heart tells me to."

"Your heart?"

He sighed. "Confound it, woman. Why is it so hard for you to allow someone to help?"

Tears stung her eyes. "I have nothing to give in return."

"Who says you have to? Sarah, these are simple everyday things that you need. It's all right to take them."

She didn't know why she struggled with this, but part of her recoiled from his gift. Surely he'd want something in return. Men always did.

He went to the pile, grabbed a few things and brought them to her. "Be so kind as to take these to the wagon."

She took them and silently headed for the double doors. She couldn't say anything at this point. On the one hand, he was acting within reason and just being kind. She was the one having a problem with it. The question was, why? On the other hand, he was challenging her. Again, why?

They put the goods into the back of the wagon, then returned for more. From the looks of it, Irving had just purchased basic supplies, far more than she normally would. All this would last for a long time if she pinched.

She faced the store. What did he say earlier? This was so she could take care of her working men? She glanced at Flint admiring his hammer again. Well, fine. She'd make him lunch every day, feed them dinner, and hope there was still enough left over to last her a spell after the Darlings left town.

By the time they loaded the wagon and prepared to leave Sarah was exhausted.

"Are you all right?" Irving asked.

"Yes, of course." In truth she could take a nap and not wake up for hours.

Irving helped her climb onto the wagon seat where she sat, her hands in her lap as he helped Lacey and Flint into the back. He climbed up beside her, took up the lines and smiled. "Are we ready?"

"Ready!" Flint cried behind them. "Let's go. I want to try out my new hammer."

"I want to make a bed for Mrs. Winkle's cousin." Lacey added.

Sarah turned slightly in her direction. "A cousin, is it?"

"Yes, all the way from Baltimore," Lacey said.

"Baltimore?" Irving smiled. "My, such a well-traveled cousin."

"I hope she doesn't get bored in Apple Blossom," Lacey said. "She's used to the good life." Lacey sighed and hugged her new doll.

Irving smiled again. "The good life?"

Sarah leaned forward and rubbed her arms to fend off a chill. Mercy, she hoped she wasn't getting sick. "It's nothing."

"She had to have heard that from somewhere," he pointed out.

"Maybe she heard Mrs. Featherstone say something. We're there often enough."

"Yes. Laundry. Which we'd best get back to." He got the horse moving, then looked her over.

"What are you doing?" She checked the front of her dress to make sure she hadn't lost a button. Speaking of which, she'd found Mrs. Winkle's eye on the kitchen floor this morning. She'd best take care of that when they got home – after the work was done, that is.

"How about the children and I take care of the laundry?" He suggested. "After all, by the time we get home, get the wagon unloaded, and the fence posts and fencing stacked, dare I say you'll be, um, tuckered out?"

She made a face at him. "Are you picking up our way of talking?"

"Perhaps a little." He glanced at her. "Sarah, you look worn out. While we're working, you can make something simple for dinner. Have a meal, then go to bed."

Her gut tightened. Why did this man have to be so nice? "We'll see."

"Not see, do."

She caught the sternness in his voice, and though it

was with his usual gentleness, she got the distinct feeling he would brook no argument. "Very well, as soon as all the supplies are put away, I'll make something simple. Thank you for all your hard work, Irving, I do appreciate it."

He smiled at her. "It's my pleasure, Sarah."

She began to wring her hands in her lap. "I'm ... sorry I put up a fuss about your generosity."

"I'm only trying to help." He stared straight ahead for a moment then smiled at her. "My father tried to help a family once. The wife was happy to accept his generosity whereas her husband balked at it. Much like you. When Father persisted, the husband threw him out of the house. Said he didn't need his help and to take his charity elsewhere."

"Goodness gracious," she said. "What happened?"

"My father came home, had a lovely dinner and after getting beaten by Sterling at several games of chess, went to bed."

She studied the road ahead, then looked at him. "And?"

He met her gaze and smiled. "And what?"

"What happened to the family your father was trying to help?"

"Father eventually did help them. The lesson was that we would run into people that needed help desperately but wouldn't accept it no matter what."

"But that's silly."

He looked her in the eyes. "That's pride."

Her throat grew thick. He might as well have slapped her. "I see."

"My father put it another way, though. He said that if you don't accept the charity of another, you still have control. By letting someone help you, one feels as if they're giving that control to the other. Do you understand?"

His voice was soft, gentle, and it was all she could do to keep from melting on the spot. "Are you saying I have to be in control?"

He leaned toward her. "Sarah, what I'm saying is it's okay to accept my generosity. You don't have to feel bad about it, and you don't have to worry that I'll ask for something in return."

She went crimson.

"That's it, isn't it? You're afraid I'll want something of you?" He glanced at the road and back. "My word, woman. I am first and foremost a gentleman."

She shut her eyes and turned away. "I never said you weren't."

"Perhaps we should leave this topic of conversation. We have work to do, after all, and Lacey has a new member of her family to show the house to."

Sarah turned to look at the children. Both were playing with their new toys. "Flint, stop hammering the flour sack."

He looked sheepishly at her, then eyed the canned goods Alma had placed in a small crate for them.

Sarah faced forward again and kept her eyes on the

road. Irving had answered her own question. Her pride was getting in the way, but she wasn't sure how to stop it.

When they reached home, he helped her and the children out of the wagon then started hauling supplies into the house. Everyone helped and soon everything was unloaded. "The children and I will take care of the rest of the laundry, hang it on the line, and bring the dried clothes inside," he declared on the front porch.

She looked into his eyes. "Thank you, Irving. For all you've done for us."

He stepped back, took off his hat and bowed. "It's been a pleasure." He straightened and left the porch.

Sarah watched him head for the pile of posts and fencing, then went inside. If only she had been Irving Darling's mail-order bride, her life would have been much different.

Chapter Ten

Irving and Flint organized their supplies for the next day, then got to work on the laundry. Irving scrubbed while the children rinsed. Flint and Lacey would do a few pieces of clothing at a time, then he'd wring out what they rinsed and hang them on the line. What dry clothes there were, he removed, folded, and put into a basket for the children to carry to the back porch.

Sarah came out of the house and looked at the basket. "My, but you've been busy."

"Those are ready for ironing," Irving called from the washtub. "We'll be done here soon enough."

Before she could comment, Chester Smythe came around the side of the house. "Howdy, folks. I thought I heard everyone back here."

Sarah went down the porch steps. "Afternoon, Mr. Smythe. What brings you here?"

"Went to town to get a few things and Alma told me you put in an order for a couple of hams, chops and bacon."

Her eyes widened. "No, I didn't ..."

"I did, sir." Irving reached into his inside vest pocket and pulled out a billfold. "How much?"

"Well, let's see," Mr. Smythe drawled. "How about eight dollars?"

"Eight dollars?" Sarah said in alarm.

Irving smiled. "Not to worry." He paid the man. "Where's the meat?"

"In my wagon. Went home and fetched it out of my smokehouse and brought it here."

Irving gave him a curt nod. "Lead on, then. Flint, we have procured some pork. Mind lending me a hand?"

"Coming!" Flint made a beeline for the front of the house.

Irving followed, Sarah on his heels. "Two whole hams, pork chops and bacon? But I never buy such things."

"All the more reason for me to purchase them. It'll be a treat." They reached the wagon and Mr. Smythe handed her a few wrapped packages.

"Do you have the bacon I ordered?" Irving asked.

"Right here." Mr. Smythe handed Sarah a few more packets.

"Land sakes," she said. "Where am I going to put all this?"

"You got a smokehouse, don't you?" Mr. Smythe asked.

"Yes, but ..." She glanced at Irving and back. "... I haven't used it much lately."

"You won't have to worry about it much longer," Irving said. "I had Alma order you an icebox." He smiled. "You do get ice delivered to town, don't you?"

"Well, yes, when there's a need. But only a few people have an icebox."

"The Featherstones get their ice delivered from Virginia City," Mr. Smythe volunteered. "But it's very expensive. If enough people wanted, they'd make a regular delivery to the entire town."

"That costs money," Sarah said with a hint of panic.

"Calm yourself," Irving soothed. "It'll be fine. You'll see." He put his hand on her shoulder and gave it a gentle squeeze before taking one of the larger packages, then another. "Thank you, Mr. Smythe. Care to walk to the smokehouse with me?" He'd looked at it the other day and, finding it empty, asked Flint about it. The boy showed him the stack of hickory wood in a shed his father used and told him what his father taught him so far about curing meat.

Sarah followed the men, looking worried. "When can I expect some ice for the icebox I don't have?"

Irving laughed. "Don't be silly, we'll store the meat in here for now." He looked at Mr. Smythe. "Unless of course you'd like to store some of this at your place until the icebox gets here."

"That's no trouble. Just put it back in the wagon." Mr. Smythe looked around the darkened interior. "Sarah, when was the last time you used this?"

She hung her head. "Not for some time."

The old man nodded sympathetically. "I understand. We all do." He left the smokehouse and waited for the others to join him.

Irving touched her elbow. "I hope you don't mind. I know the children will enjoy the meat, and you could use it."

"You're doing too much," she insisted.

"I'm not doing nearly enough." He left the smokehouse with one of the hams and hoped she followed with the bacon. He was only getting her everyday things. All of which would make her life easier and more pleasant. Why couldn't she see that? Why did she have such a hard time accepting his help?

They walked Mr. Smythe back to the wagon, returned over half the meat to the wagon bed, then said their goodbyes. He'd speak to Mr. Featherstone about ice delivery, then talk to Sterling about an icehouse for the town. They wouldn't have time to build one, but if they could persuade the captain to take on the project and get himself some help, the people of Apple Blossom could have ice during the warmer months and, once it was gone, procure some from Virginia City. If enough people wanted it, they could get it at a discount.

When Mr. Smythe left, Sarah went to the kitchen while Irving and the children returned to the laundry area. They finished their work, hung up the clothes to dry and cleaned up. "We've had a productive afternoon," Irving stated.

"No, we haven't," Flint said. "I haven't used my hammer yet."

"Trust me, lad, you'll have plenty of opportunity tomorrow. We'll rebuild that fence, then you and your sister can paint it."

Lacey smiled. "Paint?"

Irving shrugged. "Whitewash, actually. I hear you're a tyrant with paint."

She laughed and hugged her new doll.

He smiled. "I say, but have you found out her name?"

Lacey held the doll up. "Miss Penelope Parsnip."

"Parsnip," he laughed. "How did you come up with that name?"

Lacey frowned. "I didn't. Mrs. Winkle told me what it was."

His eyebrows shot up. "I beg your pardon, then." He looked at the doll. "How do you do, Miss Parsnip? You wouldn't happen to be related to Tamara Turnip, would you?"

Lacey held the doll to her ear. "She says no."

"Really? I would think she'd be familiar with the Turnips of Salisbury. No matter. Shall we head inside and see what your mother is up to?"

"Is she upset?" Flint asked.

Irving stared at the house. "I'm afraid your mother is

having a hard time accepting my generosity. She seems to think I want something in return." He'd have to do something about that, but what?

"Ma don't trust folks much," Flint said. "But we're thankful." His eyes darted to the house and back. "We haven't had this much food in a long time."

"I dare say you haven't, young man." Irving mussed the boy's hair. "It's one of the reasons I did it. And I want nothing in return, do you understand?"

The children nodded and ran into the house.

Irving went to the front of the house and looked at the piles of fencing, the new posts, the porch. It would take him at least four more days to finish everything he wanted to get done, not counting Sarah's bedroom floor. He'd have to speak to his brothers again about their departure date. It was beginning to look more and more like it would have to be postponed – especially once Letty and Cassie were factored in.

Inside he found everyone gathered around the stove. Sarah had chopped up some potatoes and had them frying in a pan. Now she was cutting slices of ham. "Whatever are you concocting?" he asked.

"Fried ham, eggs, potatoes. It's quick and it's easy."

"And filling!" Flint added, a gleam in his eye. He licked his lips and watched Sarah slice the ham. "I'll have to help you with the smokehouse."

"Yes, quite," Irving said. "We don't keep one ourselves."

"You don't?" Flint said with raised eyebrows. "Where do you keep your meat?"

Irving winked. "At the butcher's. Most every village has one."

Lacey tugged on his pants leg. "Mr. Darling?"

He bent to her. "Yes, love?"

"What's a village?"

"Didn't you ask me this before?" He looked at Sarah and shrugged. "What you call a town, in England, is called a village. Anything smaller than a village is called a hamlet."

Lacey pointed to the ham her mother was slicing. "Like that? How can people live in something so small?"

He laughed. "That, my dear pet, is a ham. A hamlet might consist of an inn, a few residents, and be located in between two villages."

Lacey whispered something to Miss Parsnip.

Irving watched her a moment then noticed a tear cutting its way down Sarah's cheek. She quickly wiped it away, then continued her slicing.

Drat the man! Why did he have to be so kind, generous and handsome? He was making it almost impossible to concentrate on what she was doing. If she wasn't careful, she was liable to slice a finger. "Children, why don't you set the table?"

Flint and Lacey headed for the hutch on the other

side of the kitchen. Irving stepped to the worktable and smiled warmly. Drat his smile too. "Need any help?"

Sarah did her best not to make eye contact. "Help the children if you'd like."

He nodded and joined them at the hutch. She listened to the clink of plates and silverware then watched the three go to the table. She and the children hadn't had this much meat in the house in ages. It was a treat, and she wanted them to enjoy it. But it was hard not to think of what Mr. Darling might want in return. She wished she didn't have such a suspicious nature and thought she was doing better over the last few days. Perhaps his intentions were true, and he didn't want anything.

A knock at the door interrupted her thoughts. "Who could that be?" She wiped her hands on her apron and went to answer it. "Captain Stanley," she said in surprise. She opened the door wide. "Come in."

"I was just passing by," he said and came through. "Alma told me you were in town, and I thought I'd check on you." He sniffed the air. "Potatoes?"

"Yes, you're welcome to stay and eat with us."

"Well, don't mind if I do. But only if there's enough." He leaned toward her. "Is there?"

She sighed. "Thanks to Mr. Darling, yes."

The captain arched one bushy eyebrow. "Which one?"

"Irving, the one working on my house. He's in the kitchen with the children." She led the way and as soon as they entered, got back to slicing the ham.

The captain took in the food, then Irving. "Looks like a feast." He scratched his head. "I was thinking of inviting you to my place for dinner tonight, but seeing as how you have all this food..." He gave Flint a pointed look.

Flint gave him a helpless shrug in return. Sarah had no idea what that was about so ignored it.

"Captain Stanley!" Lacey said. "Meet Miss Parsnip. She's Mrs. Winkle's cousin."

His eyes popped wide. "Well, will you look here. Now isn't she a pretty thing with her yellow hair? Miss Parsnip, is it? What a fine name you have." He shook the doll's hand then searched the room. "But where's Mrs. Winkle?"

"In my room, resting in her bed. She's not feeling very well. It's her eye."

Captain Stanley ran a hand over his beard. "Maybe I'd better make her an eye patch."

Lacey's face lit up. "Could you? Then she could be a pirate!"

The captain cringed. "Or work in the crow's nest. How does that sound?"

Lacey giggled and ran from the room.

The captain laughed before turning to the others. "I hope she doesn't expect an eye patch for Mrs. Winkle this very moment."

"I don't think so." Sarah brought a plate of ham to the stove and began putting it in a hot pan. It sizzled and popped and helped take her mind off Irving. Now if he would just leave, she could breathe again.

"I see the front fence is torn up. About time that got fixed." The captain looked around the room. "What are your plans for the kitchen?"

"Paint, of course," Irving said. "A lovely light green or yellow, perhaps."

"Fine choices, lad." Captain Stanley went to the kitchen table and sat in his usual spot. "Alma tells me you ordered an icebox."

"No doubt the whole town will know," Irving commented.

"It's a good thing," the captain said. "I've been trying to get ice delivered to Apple Blossom ever since I got here. If we had a proper storehouse, we could keep our own for some time. We'd just have to harvest it."

"From the lake?" Sarah asked as she turned the potatoes.

"Exactly," the captain said. He looked at Irving. "There's a small lake outside of town about a half mile off the road on your way to Bozeman. Freezes over every year and stays that way for months."

Irving nodded sagely. Sarah wondered what he was thinking, then pushed the thought aside. She'd best not think of him at all. She went to a basket on the counter, took what few eggs she had, then did a quick head count. She didn't need eggs. Ham and potatoes would do her fine. She continued making dinner as the men talked and wondered what to do for dessert. She had everything now for more cookies and could whip up a batch quick enough.

Lacey returned to the kitchen with Mrs. Winkle while Flint showed off his new hammer to the captain. It was nice having men in the house, the banter of children, the smell of good food cooking on the stove. It gave her comfort, and she wished she could hold onto the feeling forever. But in the morning, her drudgery would start again, and she would iron, then labor over the washtub until it was time to deliver the clean laundry to their owners. She hoped Mrs. Featherstone didn't complain – or short her pay – again.

When it came time to eat, everyone sat and listened as the captain gave the blessing. Flint wolfed down his potatoes, chewed his ham with relish, and gobbled up his eggs. Irving wasn't far behind him when he looked at her plate. "I say, but ... did you not get any eggs?"

"I'm fine." She poked at her potatoes and hoped he dropped it.

She should've known better. He peered at her plate again. "Would you like some of mine?"

"No, thank you." She continued eating, avoiding eye contact. Again.

"You can have my eggs, Mama," Lacey offered.

"No, sweetheart," she said. "I don't want any."

Lacey tapped her fork on her plate a few times. "Okay." She got back to eating and left it at that.

If only Irving would. "Really, Sarah, I don't need the extra egg."

She shut her eyes. "No. Thank you."

"She doesn't need an egg, lad," Captain Stanley stated.

Sarah opened her eyes. There was something in his voice she couldn't pinpoint. She hoped he didn't plan to lecture her later. When Captain Stanley offered her things, she didn't accept his generosity at first either. But the captain gave her little things; like the small sack of flour he brought the other day, not armloads of provisions as Irving had done that afternoon.

The meal over, she gathered the dishes and put them into the dry sink as the men continued to talk. Lacey and Flint wandered to their room to play, and she began heating water. She'd get the dishes done, then make some cookies.

Sarah glanced at the men as they spoke quietly and took the opportunity to slip onto the back porch. It was dusk, and she heard a night bird cry out. It was a lonely sound and made her feel the same. She hugged herself and looked at the darkening sky.

Loneliness crept into her heart, and she tried to push it away but to no avail. She was alone in her dreary little house with two small children, spongy floorboards in her bedroom and a family of skunks beneath it. She washed other people's laundry, struggled to put food on the table, and didn't have money to fix the roof or anything else in her house. Why, then, was she being such a fool? She should accept anything the Darlings offered, yet part of her wouldn't. Was it as

Irving said, that if she took his help, she'd be giving up control?

Ha! What control? Her life was *out* of control.

"Sarah?" Irving called. "I say, but what are you doing out here?" Behind her now, he put his hand on her shoulder, sending a tingle up her spine.

She swallowed hard. "Just enjoying a moment of peace and quiet before doing dishes."

"I can't say I blame you. It's been a busy day. You were supposed to be resting at this point. Flint and I can do the dishes."

She turned to face him. "Nonsense. I'll get them done, then bake a batch of cookies."

He glanced at the door. "I think the captain is making coffee."

She smiled. "Of course he is. We always have cookies and coffee when he comes."

"A partnership, is it?"

She sighed wearily. "Something like that."

"Life is easier with two rather than one."

"So says the Good Book," she said. "I'm lucky, then. With the children that's three." She hurried into the house and got to work.

He followed, went to the dry sink, then took a dishrag from a nail pounded into the wall. "I'll check the water."

Before she could protest, he grabbed the kettle, poured water into the sink's washtub and checked the temperature with his finger. "Hot enough." He grabbed the box of Snow Flakes off the windowsill, added some to the tub, then swished the water around with his hand.

Sarah watched his movements and tried to make herself move but couldn't. Instead, she stared at the handsome Englishman as he prepared to do her dishes.

"Mama?" Lacey asked as she entered the kitchen.

Sarah sighed in relief and turned around. "Yes, sweetheart?"

"Will you read Miss Parsnip and me a story?"

Captain Stanley smiled. "Of course, she will, lass."

Sarah shook her head. "Captain, I have work ..."

"Being a mother *is* work," he said. "Go ahead. Read to the child. We have it all in hand here."

Irving smiled at her. "We'll even brave the cookies."

Her eyes widened. Though she knew Captain Stanley could bake a batch, she wasn't so sure about Irving.

Lacey grabbed her hand. "Come on, Mama. Miss Parsnip and Mrs. Winkle are waiting."

Sarah sighed in defeat and let Lacey drag her into the children's bedroom. For the first time in a very long time, she sat down and relaxed while others did the work for her.

Chapter Eleven

"There, that looks fine." Irving and Flint stepped back to admire their work. The new fence was sturdy but needed whitewashing. "I think it's time to call in the other troops."

"Lacey's not a troop. She's a six-year-old." Flint crossed his arms. "I can do the whitewashing."

"It will go faster with two," Irving pointed out.

"She'll make a mess. You'll see."

"Probably," Irving agreed. "But at least it's only whitewash." He picked up the brushes he'd purchased that morning at Alma's store. "Between the two of you, you'll be done in no time."

"Well, will you look at that?" Sarah came down the porch steps. "What a lovely picket fence." She wiped her hands on her apron and went to the gate. "Good job, Flint."

"Thanks, Ma, but Mr. Darling did some of the work." Flint grinned.

Irving smiled at Sarah. She looked better than she did the other day – she had some color in her cheeks. Amazing what enough food will do for a person. "I admit I did help."

She smiled. "Lacey is looking forward to helping."

Flint groaned. "Does she have to?"

"Yes." Sarah went through the gate to join them. "It's so nice to have something new."

"Freshens the whole place up," Irving commented. They stood next to each other, and he tried not to stand too close. She smelled of Snow Flakes, an all-purpose soap flake you could do laundry with, dishes, you name it. The new box he'd purchased at Alma's had a faint scent of lemon. He noticed her hair hadn't escaped its pins yet, and she had a rosy glow to her cheeks. Gad, what was he going to do? She was getting under his skin and into his heart.

"What's next?" she asked, pulling him from his thoughts.

"Paint the inside. My brothers will be here in the next day or two to look at the floor in your bedroom."

"All of them?"

"Yes."

She wiped her hands on her apron again. At least she wasn't wringing them. "Fine. I'll be sure to make a big batch of cookies."

"You don't have to worry about them, but you do need to figure out where you're going to sleep."

"I can sleep in the children's room." She looked at the house and smiled. "Maybe after the place is all fixed up, I … can sell it."

"Mama," Flint said in surprise. "No!"

"But dearest, wouldn't you like to live in town?"

"No," he said, shaking his head.

"So you want to keep sharing a room with your sister?" Irving asked.

Flint's jaw dropped.

Irving nodded. "Yes, that's a problem, isn't it? Becoming a man and sharing a room with Lacey, Mrs. Winkle, and Miss Parsnip."

Flint's eyes widened. "I didn't think of that."

"If everything works out," Irving went on. "You could have your own room at a new place. Have all your own things in it and no little sister."

Flint's jaw dropped again, and he grabbed his mother's skirt. "Is that true?"

"W-well," she stammered, "that depends on how big the new place is."

"Perhaps we should inquire after the millinery shop," Irving suggested. "You could take in laundry, mending, and even make clothes to sell." He looked over her dress. "You're certainly talented enough."

"Um, thank you. But who would buy this place?"

He shrugged. "I'm not sure, but the best person to talk to would be the captain. Maybe someone from

Virginia City would like to live in a smaller community."

She nodded, eyes wary.

He patted her shoulder. "Let's not worry about it now. We'll finish the house, then you can decide."

"But I want my own room," Flint whined.

She closed her eyes a moment then stared at Irving. "Thanks."

He grinned sheepishly. "Sorry, but at least he likes the idea."

She nodded again and headed for the gate. "Dinner is almost ready. You can clean up out here after you've eaten."

"Jolly good." Irving gathered their tools and headed for the porch.

"What do we do with all the old fencing?" Flint asked as he followed.

Irving smiled. "I'm sure it will make a lovely fire."

Flint caught up to him. "Can I light it?"

He stopped and arched an eyebrow at the boy. "You sound eager. We'll see." He set the tools down and headed into the house. "Mmm, something smells good."

In the kitchen, Sarah was stirring a pot. "Sit down, it's almost ready."

"What does 'it' consist of?"

"Beef stew, thanks to you." She opened the oven and took out a fresh loaf of bread.

Irving took a good sniff, glad he'd purchased some stew meat for her. "My word, what a delightful smell."

She smiled and set the loaf on the worktable, then took out a second loaf. "Also thanks to you, I'm caught up and had time to bake this afternoon." She turned to the pot and gave it another stir before moving it to the other side of the stove. "Flint, go fetch your sister."

"Sure, Ma." He took off, leaving them alone.

Irving cleared his throat. "Sarah, we can inquire about the millinery shop tomorrow."

She put the lid back on the pot. "There's no need."

"Why not? Aren't you curious what it has to offer?" He joined her at the stove. "At least look at it. That way, you can make a better decision about this place."

Her eyes fixed on the stove. "I don't know."

"I know it means change, but it would be for the better. The building is perfect for the three of you." He went to the table lest he take her in his arms. "Think about it. I can speak to Mr. Featherstone if you decide to have a peek."

She hinted at a smile. "You know, even when the shop was open, I never went inside. There was no need. I couldn't afford a new hat."

"Did the proprietress leave because she lost her husband in the, um, incident?"

She shook her head. "No, Mrs. O'Halloran lost Mr. O'Halloran to influenza a couple of years before. He was a tailor in Omaha before they came west."

"So the place has always had something to do with clothing." He rubbed his chin a few times. "Maybe you could speak with Alma about selling dresses in there. That would free up room in her store for other goods."

"She orders things special from Weaver Dressmakers and Millinery. I'm not sure how it all works."

He shrugged. "Like I said, it doesn't hurt to ask." He went to the hutch. "Shall I set the table?"

Her shoulders slumped as she stared at him. "Thank you."

Irving smiled. "At least you're willing to let me take a crack at such a menial chore." He began taking bowls from the hutch. "It's a privilege, you know, doing these things for you."

She gaped at him. "What?"

He nodded. "Mm, yes. You're made of better stuff than I am – alone out here with two children to take care of." He faced her, a stack of bowls in his hands. "I am honored to serve." He brought the dishes to the table and set them down.

She backed into the stove and jumped. "Oh!"

He was at her side in an instant. "Careful now. Don't burn yourself."

She met his gaze, her lips parted, and it was all he could do not to kiss her. "Sorry, I'm clumsy."

"Not at all. Preoccupied, perhaps. That's my fault." He realized his hands were on her arms and let go. "Carry on." He hurried back to the hutch and took silverware from a drawer. He wanted to kiss her, but she wasn't ready for … egad, what was he thinking? They weren't in any sort of relationship, and he shouldn't be thinking as if they were. Yes, he'd like to hold her, kiss her, but that ... he shook his head. "Concentrate, man," he whispered to himself. "You're leaving."

Irving brought the silverware to the table and began to set it. The children entered the kitchen (thank goodness) and joined him. "I'll get the napkins," Lacey announced.

"And I'll get the glasses." Flint headed for the hutch. Irving kept quiet as Sarah gave the pot another stir, looking at anything but him. Had she picked up on his intentions? Wait a minute, what intentions? His only intention was to finish her house, then head back to England!

He glanced her way, made sure she wasn't looking, then knocked his head a few times with his hand. "Think of what you're doing."

"What?"

Irving froze as Lacey stood beside him. "Nothing. Talking to myself." He took the napkins she offered and put one at each place setting. Flint brought the glasses and did the same. Now that the table was set, he needed something to keep him from doing something he'd regret. Brushing his hand against Sarah's, for example, or pulling her into his arms, or ... oh blast! Is this how it happened to Conrad? But no, his brother told him it came from spending time with Cassie.

Well, dash it all. How could he avoid spending time with Sarah and the children? It was impossible. At least

Cassie went to work every day. So did Sarah, only he was here with her.

He turned, went into the parlor, and sat on the sofa. It was worn and had seen better days.

Lacey joined him with Miss Parsnip. "Whatcha doing?" she asked.

He smiled at her. "Thinking."

"About what?"

He looked at her doll. "I'm wondering if Miss Parsnip and Mrs. Winkle would like to read me a story."

She laughed. "They can't, silly."

"Why not?"

"They can't read."

Irving smiled warmly. "Oh, dear, that is a problem. I guess we'd better eat dinner, then."

She laughed, left the sofa, and ran into the kitchen.

Irving took a deep breath and tried to brace himself for another wonderful evening with Sarah and the children. If this kept up, either Phileas or Conrad might be the one worrying about taking over the title and estate.

Sarah poked at her food, took small bites, and did her best not to look at Irving. He sat across the table next to Lacey and her dolls. She smiled every time he spoke to the three and noticed how he treated Miss Parsnip and Mrs. Winkle as if they were real. Lacey loved it. Despite his kindness and generosity, she still couldn't afford to get attached to this man. He and his brothers were leaving and that was that. However, it was growing hard not to.

"So, we'll whitewash the fence tomorrow, Ma," Flint informed her, sounding very grown up. "Then we plan to paint. We'll take the furniture out of the house just like Billy and Conrad did for Sheriff Laine."

Sarah fixed her eyes on him to keep from staring at Irving – and lost that battle when he chuckled. She looked at him as her heart warmed and was lost.

"You're the keenest worker I've ever met," Irving commented. "Anyone would want to have you as an employee, young man."

Flint smiled and got back to eating. Sarah noticed how happy her son had been the last day or two. And why not? He had a full belly. Shame crept into her cheeks. She'd been trying to survive, rationing food. But it was either ration the food from time to time, or not eat at all at others. Until ...

"Sarah?" Irving said, voice soft. "Is something the matter? You're quite flushed."

Her hand went to her cheek, and she rubbed it. "It's from cooking. It's warm in here."

He looked around the kitchen. "You're right, it is. We should eat outside tomorrow evening."

Her heart skipped a beat. "You plan on staying for dinner again?"

Now he blushed. "I admit I like your cooking. And it's quieter here than at the hotel – I don't have to fight

Oliver and Wallis for the last biscuit. They adore them, you know."

"I didn't." She concentrated on her food and hoped he got back to eating. If she conversed with the man, she'd have to look at him, and that would only send her belly into somersaults and her heart to fluttering.

"If I can get my brothers organized, would tomorrow work?"

She swallowed hard and looked at him. A tingle went up her spine. "Yes. Fine." She took another bite of food, eyes glued to her bowl.

"I say, but you're quiet this evening," he commented.

"Am I?" She shoved a piece of potato into her mouth.

"Is anything wrong?" he asked, brow furrowed.

"What makes you ask?"

"You are quiet, Ma," Flint added. "Are you tired? Do you need to go to bed?"

"An excellent question," Irving said. "Do you?"

She set down her spoon. "No. I do not. I'm fine, just a little warm. Now will you please finish your dinner?"

"What's for dessert?" Lacey asked with a grin.

"Never you mind. I want you to eat everything in your bowl, young lady."

Lacey looked around the table. "But what's for dessert?"

Sarah let go an impatient sigh. "Lacey ..."

Irving gasped. "Look, Miss Parsnip and Mrs. Winkle finished their food. They're waiting on you."

Lacey also gasped, then gaped at her dolls. "They

have, haven't they?" She looked at her food then took a huge bite of stew.

Irving winked at Sarah. "I dare say, those dolls were hungry."

She smiled as her heart warmed. "They certainly were. Looks like they'll get dessert."

Lacey gasped again and ate faster.

"Slow down," Irving advised. "Before you choke."

Lacey giggled and kept eating.

Flint held up his bowl. "Look, Ma, I finished."

She sighed and sat back in her chair. "Good job. You'll get dessert too." She eyed Irving's plate. "I don't know about you. You haven't finished yours."

He gave the children a sheepish look. "Whoops."

She finished her own dinner then left her chair. As soon as she did, Lacey held up both hands. "I'm dwone!" she said, mouth full.

"Lacey, ladies do not talk with their mouths full." She gathered everyone's dishes and took them to the dry sink. "Irving, would you like some coffee?"

He left his chair and joined her at the stove. "I can make it. What is for dessert anyway?"

She shrugged helplessly. "Leftover cookies from yesterday."

He took a step closer. "That's quite all right. None of us mind. A sweet is a sweet as far as I'm concerned."

"Wouldn't you rather be at the hotel enjoying some of Dora's pie?" She grabbed the kettle off the stove and headed for the back door.

Irving followed. "I'm sure you make a good pie."

She went outside to the pump. As soon as she reached it, he took the kettle from her. "What are you doing?"

"Filling this, silly." He began pumping water into the kettle. "When was the last time you baked a pie?"

Sarah laughed. "Is that a hint?"

He smiled at her. "Could be."

"And what kind of pie are you hinting at?"

"Any, really. Though I am partial to cherry. You wouldn't happen to have any preserves on hand, would you?"

"No, but I know who does. The captain."

He finished filling the kettle and put the lid back on. "Really? The man is a virtual storehouse."

"He is. He stocks up on things every time he goes to Bozeman or Virginia City. Then he gives them to people in need. Like me." She blushed and headed for the back door. She knew he would follow, and by the time she returned to the kitchen, maybe her cheeks would have gone from red to pink.

Inside he put the kettle on the hottest part of the stove. "Shall I make the coffee now?"

She sighed. Thank goodness he wasn't pressing things. "Sure. You know where everything is."

He smiled and headed for the larder to fetch the coffee. While he busied himself with that, she got down to the business of doing dishes.

The children had disappeared and were probably in

their room, playing. When Sarah dried the last dish, the coffee had begun to boil. "I'll get the cookie jar."

"Jolly good," Irving called after her. He sat at the kitchen table, and she noticed he had an odd look on his face. Pensive?

As soon as the coffee was done, she poured them each a cup, brought the cream and sugar to the table and sat.

"Shall I call the children?" he asked.

Sarah shook her head. "Let's enjoy a few moments of peace and quiet first." She took a cookie from the jar and bit into it.

Irving did the same and watched her. There was that look again. What was it? Drat, who knew what he was thinking?

He took another cookie for himself. "I've been wondering ..."

She stopped chewing and looked at him. "About what?"

"This place. I think I'll speak to Mr. Featherstone tomorrow. About the millinery shop." He bit into his cookie.

Her heart stopped. This again! "Are you planning on buying it?" She sounded terse. "I'm sorry."

"Don't be. You're nervous about it. Anyone can see that."

"I have good reason to be. Please don't push me on this."

"Well, you may not want to look at the millinery shop, but out of curiosity I do. I'd very much like to see what's there. If you don't want it, perhaps it would suit Jean. She's talented enough to open a bakery. I'm sure it wouldn't take much to convert the place."

Sarah smiled. "An undertaker-baker. My goodness."

"She must make a living too. And let's face it, no one's needed an undertaker around here in quite some time."

She nodded. "That's true. And I admit it's a good idea. But don't you think Jean would have already thought of it?"

"When has she had the time?" He laughed. "My brothers and I have kept her busy ever since our arrival."

"Cooking and baking?" she teased.

"Something like that. Dora seems to be enjoying herself."

"She loves to cook. Always has. I'm not sure which she likes better, cooking or reading." She wrapped her hands around her cup and enjoyed the warmth. "I don't bake nearly as much as they do."

"You're not cooking and baking for six men. Only two." He winked.

Sarah smiled. "Flint adores you. But I'm sure you already knew that."

"He looks up to me, that's all. Like Billy does Conrad."

"But Billy has a father. Flint doesn't. There's a difference, you know."

"Yes, I'm aware. You're worried he'll be heartbroken when we leave, is that it?"

She nodded as her chest tightened. "I don't want them to lose someone else ..."

He came around the table as her first tear fell. She didn't know where it came from, it was just there. "There now, don't cry. Everything will be all right, you'll see." He pulled a handkerchief from his pocket and handed it to her.

Sarah took it and dabbed her eyes. "I'm sorry, I don't know what's the matter with me."

He put his hand on her shoulder and gave it a gentle squeeze. "You're exhausted, that's what's the matter. You need a few days' rest."

She shook her head. "I'm afraid I can't. I have work to do, you know that."

He bent to her, his mouth near her ear. "What I know is that there's a better way. Won't you investigate it with me?"

Sarah looked him in the eyes. "And if I did, then what? You won't always be here to help us, will you? You're leaving."

Irving closed his eyes and nodded. "That's true. But while I'm here, allow me to do what I can. Please?"

Sarah took a breath, held it, and finally nodded. She hoped she didn't regret it.

Chapter Twelve

I rving sighed in relief. He didn't want Sarah to see how much he wanted her to look at the millinery shop. He'd hoped telling her that Jean might be interested would prompt her to act. It didn't, but a simple "please" did. Thank goodness.

He sipped his coffee, enjoyed his cookies, then looked toward the parlor. "Shouldn't we call the children?"

Sarah let out a breath. Good heavens, was she nervous? "Yes. I'll fetch them." She left the table and went to the parlor.

Irving exhaled himself and drummed his fingers on the tabletop. Her words stung but were unfortunately true. He and his brothers *would* be leaving soon, and Flint and Lacey would once again be left without a man around. He'd have to speak to Captain Stanley and see if he could visit the Crawfords more often. They needed him, and though Irving suspected the captain knew this, he also knew the man had a heart for all of Apple Blossom's residents.

He arched an eyebrow. "What does he do all day?" He turned in his chair to see if Sarah was coming back. He'd have to ask her.

When she returned with the children, Flint and Lacey ran to the table and took their seats. "I want my cookie now," Lacey stated.

Irving noticed she didn't bring her dolls. Had Sarah told her not to? "Some cookies are better the second day. Did you know that?"

Lacey shook her head. "I just know they taste good any day." She smiled expectantly at her mother. "Can I have two?"

Sarah managed a weary smile. "Of course, you can." She took two from the jar for Lacey, two for Flint, then offered the jar to him. "Would you like another?"

Irving peeked in the jar. "Oh dear, it looks as if we've wiped them out." He looked at the children and smiled. "Perhaps the three of us could try our hand at baking tomorrow?"

Flint's eyes lit up. "Does that mean we get to eat them all?"

"Absolutely not." Sarah put the lid on the jar. "You'll get a bellyache."

"Aw, Ma. I will not." He took a huge bite of cookie.

Sarah shook her head in dismay. "I give up."

Irving took her hand. "Cheer up. We'll do the baking tomorrow. You can take a nap."

She laughed. "You are so amusing."

"In all seriousness, Sarah," he said gently. "You should rest. Let us do some of the work."

Her shoulders slumped. "I did say I'd let you help me, didn't I?"

He slowly nodded. "You did indeed."

"Fine, I concede. You and the children can do the baking tomorrow. But that doesn't mean they get out of whitewashing the fence." She narrowed her eyes at them. "Understand?"

Lacey giggled. "Yes, Mama."

Flint nodded and shoved the rest of his cookie into his mouth.

"Now that that's settled," Irving said. "I think I'll get another cup of coffee." He went to the stove. "Want some more?"

Sarah retook her seat. "Please."

He brought the pot, poured her a cup, and noticed how frail she looked. Though getting enough food had brought color to her cheeks, she hadn't gained any weight yet. He hoped she did. She could use some, considering the way her clothes fit. "We should pay another visit to the general store. I think you should make yourself a new dress for the dance."

"Dance?" She blinked a few times in confusion.

"Great Scott, woman," he said in surprise, returning the coffee pot to the stove. "The dance Dora, Cassie, Letty, and Jean thought up? No, wait, I believe Alma came up with the idea first."

Sarah brushed hair from her face. "Oh, yes, I did hear mention of that." She looked at her drab grayish work dress. "I don't have it in me to make a new dress. Besides, I can't ..." She looked at him and snapped her mouth shut. "Let's not talk about it."

"I want to go to a dance," Lacey said. "Can we, Mama?"

Sarah's eyes filled with apprehension as she looked at her.

Irving went behind Sarah and rested his hands on her shoulders. "I think we should all go. How often do you have a chance to dress up and celebrate?"

"What are we celebrating?" Flint asked. "Do I have to dress up?" He shoved half of his second cookie into his mouth.

"It's a chance to speak with people in town you don't often see. Especially living out here." He gave Sarah's shoulders a squeeze and let go. To hold her any longer would be improper. He paced the kitchen instead. "There will be music, food, and who knows what sort of other entertainments?"

Lacey's face contorted in confusion. "What's enter-tain-ments?"

"Anything other than dancing. Wallis knows how to juggle, for instance."

Flint's face lit up. "So does Captain Stanley! If we get our lessons done in time, he juggles for us."

"Well, well – is there nothing that man can't do?" Irving smiled at the children, then winked at Sarah. Her eyes filled with ... Great Scott, was it admiration? His chest swelled. "I believe the dance will be held in a couple of weeks. Perhaps less. I should have paid more attention when Conrad was talking about it."

"We all have our minds on other things," Sarah stated, eyes on the table.

Irving's heart went out to her. He knew she was still scared about the possibility of change, even if it was for the better. But there was only so much he could do. She was the one that had to put one foot in front of the other to make it happen.

"It's almost time for bed, children," Sarah announced. "Would you like me to read you a story?"

"Let Mr. Darling do it!" Lacey begged. "Please?" She blinked at him a few times.

His heart melted. He sighed and glanced at Sarah. "How can I resist a look like that?"

"Practice," she quipped. "I had to."

Irving laughed. "I have no doubt. Does Lacey know how adorable she is?"

Sarah held a finger to her lips. "I try not to let her."

He laughed again. "Oh, very well. Where's the book?"

"I'll get it!" Lacey scrambled out of her chair and ran to the parlor.

Irving smiled at Sarah. "Your children are delightful. I daresay I'll miss them when I'm gone."

She looked at him, her eyes filling with something

else now. Perhaps he shouldn't have said anything. "They'll miss you too. You know they will."

"Yes, so you said." He glanced at Flint and back. "I'll try to make it as easy on them as I can."

She closed the distance between them. "Irving," she said quietly. "I don't see how that can be done. The more time they spend with you …"

"I know," he said, voice just as low. "But I must finish what I've started here."

She nodded. They both knew the work had to be done. Speaking of work, Irving went to the door of her bedroom and opened it. "What are you doing?" she asked.

He took a good whiff, caught the scent of skunks, and waved his hand in front of his nose. "They're still down there, I see."

"I'm afraid so." She stepped away. "I don't know what you can do about them."

"We'll figure something out. In the meantime, are you all right sleeping in there?"

She shrugged. "I've grown accustomed to it. But if anything scares them, it will be unbearable."

He looked sheepishly at her. "As in, if any of my brothers scare them?"

She smiled. "Exactly. Do be careful when you tackle the floor."

Lacey reentered the kitchen holding a large book. "Here, Mr. Darling."

Sarah took one look at the book and shut her eyes. "Irving, it's all yours."

He took the book from the child and read the title. "*The Princess and the Pirate* by C.I. Sayer." He smiled. "I believe Oliver has read this."

Flint left his chair. "It's full of all kinds of adventure stories. The captain has a copy too."

"Does he?" Irving said. "And did he buy you this copy?"

The children nodded, eyes bright.

Irving smiled at Sarah. "Shall we retire to the parlor then?"

She took a deep breath as if to brace herself, then nodded.

Irving tried to ignore the action but knew something was wrong. It was as if she didn't want to be in the same room with him. Should he back off and return to the hotel in the evenings for dinner? But he was growing so attached to the little family, the question was, could he?

The next day, Irving showed up extra early and strolled into the kitchen. Sarah stared at him then remembered to turn the bacon. "What are you doing here?"

"I came to make cookies," he stated happily.

She blinked a few times, her mouth moving but nothing came out. She was flummoxed.

"Don't look so surprised," he said. "I did say that the children and I would take care of the baking today."

"You … did," she managed. "I didn't think you'd show up this early to make them. The children aren't even out of bed yet."

"Shall I wake the tykes?" He leaned against the door jamb. "I could sprinkle water on their faces. I used to do that to Conrad. It drove him mad." He grinned devilishly and waggled his eyebrows.

"You'll do no such thing." She turned the rest of the bacon. "Have you had your breakfast?"

"No, as a matter of fact – I came here straightaway." He joined her at the stove. "Smells good."

She glanced at him and smiled. "As long as you don't use water, you can wake the children." She gave him a warning glare, then cracked an egg into a pan.

"Right. No water," he said. "I'll tickle them instead." Before she could say anything, he was gone.

Sarah took a deep breath, let it out, then turned her potatoes as the egg fried. Flint would be the first one at the table, so she got his plate ready. By the time the egg was done Flint was sitting in his usual spot. "Mr. Darling didn't sprinkle water on you, did he?" She set the plate in front of him.

"No, but what's he doing here so early?" Flint snuck a chunk of potato off his plate and popped it in his mouth.

Lacey was next to come to the table. "Mr. Darling tickled me!" She took her seat. "Mama, I'm hungry."

"Good, because I made a big breakfast." She fixed Lacey's plate and set it in front of her. She then fixed one for Irving, and one for herself. Soon everyone was seated, she said the blessing, and they began to eat.

"We're baking cookies right after this," Irving stated. "What kind should we make?"

"Molasses!" Flint said, waving his fork around.

"Stop that," Sarah scolded. "You'll poke someone's eye out." She took a bite of egg and tried to remember where she put her recipe for molasses cookies. Unless Irving was a master baker and knew some recipe by heart, which she doubted, she wouldn't have to look.

As if reading her thoughts, he leaned toward her. "Have you a cookery book?"

She smiled and leaned toward him. "Maybe. Why, are you in need of one?"

"Could be. Haven't made molasses cookies in a long time."

She smiled again. "As in ever?"

"Right." He got back to eating.

She sighed. "Yes, I have one. But I'm not sure my recipe for molasses cookies is in it."

"Know it by heart, do you? You're one of those cooks." He gave her an exaggerated wink.

"What is that supposed to mean?" If she could get away with it, she'd flick a potato at him.

"It means you don't need a cookery book or recipe. Cakes, pies, cookies and all sorts of confections flow from your fingertips into the mixing bowl and –"

"Oh, please," she said, pinching the bridge of her nose. "Don't be ridiculous."

He chuckled, finished his eggs and looked at the children. "Your mother will be very nervous letting us take over the kitchen. How can we alleviate her fears?"

"Leave-ee-ate?" Lacey repeated.

Flint shook his head. "How should we know? We don't cook."

"This will be exciting then." Irving laughed softly, and the children flew into hysterics.

Sarah didn't bother to scold them – let them have their fun. They were happy with Irving, and it was a shame he would be gone soon. But there was nothing she could do about it.

After breakfast, she cleared away the dishes, went into her room and began to sort through a stack of books on her nightstand. "I know it's in here somewhere."

Irving stood in the doorway. "So you wrote it on a scrap of paper then stuck it in one of those?" He nodded at the stack.

"Something like that. I wrote it down for Jean and forgot to give it to her."

"When was that?"

She stopped and sighed. "About two years ago." With a helpless shrug she got back to searching. "You must think me slothful."

"Not at all." He stepped into the room. "Is there anything I can do to help?"

"There's another stack of books on the top shelf in the armoire. You could go through those."

"Right, then." Sarah watched him open the armoire and began to leaf through the first book. She wanted to stay and supervise, but where would the fun be? The children wanted to make cookies with Irving unfettered. She just hoped they didn't destroy the kitchen doing so.

"Ha!"

She jumped, a hand to her chest. "Good heavens. Did you find it?"

He waved a folded piece of paper in the air. "By Jove, I have!" He crossed the room and handed it to her.

She unfolded the paper. "Yes, this is it." She handed it back. "Think you can handle it?"

Irving studied the recipe. "As long as I get the measurements right, of course." He folded the recipe and put it in his vest pocket. "It can't be that hard."

"It's not, so long as you follow everything correctly. It's the baking you might have trouble with."

He looked panicked, and she wasn't sure if he was playing or not. "How so?"

"You want the temperature just right. Too hot and you burn the cookies. Then of course there's the timing."

"So there's a science to it." He patted his vest pocket. "Well, so long as I don't burn down the house or the cookies, we'll be fine."

"My goodness," she laughed. "As if I haven't enough trouble."

"Oh, ye of little faith."

She crossed her arms. "Let me put it another way. Don't let Flint burn down my house."

His eyebrows shot up in alarm. "Perish the thought."

She followed him into the kitchen and helped him gather ingredients. They put everything on the worktable before Irving went to fetch the children. She hoped Flint didn't get bored and start insisting they work on the fence. But if Irving promised he'd get a cookie out of the first batch, he wouldn't pester him.

As if on cue, Flint ran into the kitchen. "Are we ready to make cookies?"

"I believe so," Irving said. "Are you ready to clean the kitchen once we're done?"

Flint's face screwed up. "What? You didn't say anything about having to clean up."

"My young fellow, did we not clean up after working on the fence? Did we not clean up after working on the front and back porches?"

Flint thought a moment. "Oh, yeah, we did."

"So, isn't it logical that we'd clean up the kitchen after we've worked in it?" Irving arched an eyebrow and waited for his answer.

Sarah's heart melted at their exchange. It was a simple thing, but Irving was so good with Flint and Lacey that ... she turned away as tears stung her eyes. She shouldn't torture herself like this. She married Caleb Crawford shortly after getting off the stage all those years ago. She had two wonderful children because of that union, and though Caleb was gone now, their life wasn't so bad.

Still, at least she had company then, someone to talk to, someone she could count on. For the most part.

She supposed she could count on Irving while he was here, but how long would that be? She was surprised she'd warmed up to him as much as she had, considering her suspicious nature. But he had a gentle way about him and was hard to say no to.

"Would you like me to fill the kettle?"

Sarah shook herself. "What?"

Irving stepped toward her, a smile on his face. "The kettle. I'll fill it, shall I?"

"Oh, yes. Thank you." Her hand to her chest, she looked at the cold iron sitting on the shelf beneath the worktable. She grabbed it and put it on the stove. "I have my morning chores to do, then deliveries to make."

He noticed the iron and nodded. "We'll try not to get in your way."

She nodded back and went into the bedroom, where she kept the clean baskets of laundry. She would iron and fold everything, put the baskets in her wheelbarrow and take them to town.

She took a pair of trousers from the first basket, laid them on the ironing board, then went to check the iron. As soon as she thought it was hot enough, she brought it back to her room and got to work. Each time she reheated the iron, she stopped a moment and watched Irving and the children make cookie dough. She marveled at how well-behaved Flint and Lacey were and wished they'd act that way when *she* was making cookies.

Half the time it was all she could do to keep them out of the dough.

Soon they had their first batch in the oven and Irving looked like he'd just won a prize. "Eureka! We did it!"

Lacey jumped up and down. "Hooray!"

Flint looked at the small clock on the shelf by the dry sink. "How long does it take? I'm hungry."

"You are not," Sarah said. "You just had breakfast."

"I'm hungry for cookies!" He grinned.

Sarah glanced at Irving who was staring at her, a silly smile on his face. "What?"

He shook his head. "I ... was just struck by ..." He shrugged. "... how beautiful you are."

Sarah gasped, plucked the iron off the stove with a hot pad and hurried back to the bedroom.

Chapter Thirteen

"**W**hat's the matter with you?" Phileas asked at breakfast the next day.

Irving looked at his brother and sighed. "It's nothing."

Phileas studied him, eyebrows raised in curiosity. "I'd say it's something, judging from the look on your face." He leaned forward. "You don't look yourself. Is it because of Sterling?"

Irving glanced at Oliver and Wallis. Conrad had already left for Cassie's, and Sterling was off to Letty's. "I ... well ... it's the Widow Crawford."

"What about her?" Phileas asked.

Oliver smiled. "You remember the Widow Crawford, Phileas. Blonde, blue eyes, thin." His smile grew. "Pretty."

Irving rolled his eyes. "I need to know if you chaps can help me with something."

"Her floor?" Oliver said. "Yes, of course."

"Didn't you mention it needed replacing?" Wallis asked.

"It does." Irving buttered his toast. "And in order to get it done in a timely manner, we'll have to work together."

"I don't see a problem," Phileas said. "I'm sure Conrad and Sterling can tear themselves away from their ladies long enough to help."

"And what about you?" Irving took a bite and chewed.

"I'm available. Conrad is all but finished with Cassie's house. When do you need me?"

"Today. I'd like to pick up some paint, but I know you'll want to look at the place first." He sipped his coffee. If he kept talking about the work, maybe he'd forget about the notion of kissing Sarah. It was one of the reasons he didn't show up early again. It was safer if he had others around while working at her place. He was less likely to do something stupid. He couldn't afford to get involved with her any more than he already was. He had the title and estate to think of. He had his duty.

"When are you heading over?" Phileas asked.

"Right after breakfast. We can walk."

Phileas sat back in his chair and thought about it. "Are there painting supplies already there?"

"We'll need more brushes. I bought a couple, but the children will be using them to finish whitewashing the fence."

"That's right, she has two little ones." Phileas smiled. "How have they been to work around?"

"Fine. Flint is a big help. I even bought him his own hammer."

"What?" Oliver said with a laugh. "That's brave. Has he smashed anything he shouldn't yet?"

Irving smiled. "Not yet, thank goodness."

Oliver sighed theatrically. "That's a relief."

Irving smiled again. "Yes. The little tyke is a good worker. Like Billy, though not as efficient."

"Amazing what a year can do," Wallis said. "Isn't Billy older?"

Irving nodded as Sarah's face flashed before him. How was he going to stop thinking about her? Every time he did his chest warmed and an odd peace permeated his soul.

"Irving," Phileas said. "You've got that funny look on your face again."

He shook his head. "I've a lot on my mind, that's all."

"I dare say you have," Wallis said. "What with Conrad and Sterling both on the marital hook."

"Wallis, that's quite enough," Phileas scolded. "Who knows, love could strike you next."

"Me?" Wallis laughed. "What about Irving? He's the one working alongside the pretty widow."

Oliver rolled his eyes. "He has the estate and title to worry about. Not to mention Mother and Father."

Irving cringed. "Don't bring them up. I'm already

having nightmares about what Mother will do upon our return."

Wallis shuddered, followed by Phileas. Oliver, on the other hand, took another serving of fried potatoes. As the youngest, he had the least to worry about. He was, after all, the last in line to inherit the title and estate. "I don't know what all the fuss is about," he said. "Mother will understand."

Irving, Wallis, and Phileas looked at one another, then laughed.

Oliver's eyebrows shot up. "What did I say?"

Irving left the table first. "Coming, Phileas?"

"Of course." Phileas took one last look at Oliver, shook his head, then looked pointedly at Wallis. "Any one of us could be next. Remember that."

Wallis reached for a muffin. "Then it's a good thing Irving has it all in hand, eh?"

A chill went up Irving's spine. "Let us hope I do." He motioned Phileas toward the hotel lobby, and they left.

They stopped by Alma's first and got some samples of paint, more brushes and other supplies. Then they began the trek to Sarah's house. Phileas breathed deeply a few times. "I like the mornings here, don't you? They're different than England's."

"The air seems fresher, somehow." Irving also took a deep breath. "You can smell the dust of the road, the dew, and of course the apples. Have you been harvesting in the evenings?"

"Yes. Dora and I helped twice after dinner these past

few days." He smiled. "Pray tell, what were your evenings like?"

Irving couldn't help but smile. "Pleasant. I must admit, it's been nice seeing how the widow's little family lives. They're poor as church mice yet seem happy. Well, the children do, but ..."

"Yes?" Phileas prompted.

"They hunger."

Phileas stopped. "What?"

He nodded. "I've bought them food, supplies, and the poor woman wanted to refuse the gift. I dare say her pride will starve them to death."

"Are the children well?"

"Yes, though Flint confided in me he's hungry most of the time." He looked at Phileas and sighed. "She has food, but not enough."

"Dear me, that is a problem. What will you do?"

"I'm trying to talk her into selling her place and buying the millinery shop in town. She could do mending, make clothes to sell. Perhaps become the town dressmaker."

"Does Apple Blossom need one?" Phileas asked. "I know the women in town are excited about the dance – it gives them an excuse to make new frocks. They seem capable enough."

"And when the town grows?"

Phileas laughed. "I'm not sure it ever will."

Irving stopped. "But if it does? Think about it, brother. Apple Blossom could be something special." He studied their surroundings. They hadn't gotten past the orchards yet. "The town sells apples, but what if they could make something else from them?"

"Yes, but what?"

"We should speak to the captain. These orchards are mature and, as far as I know, the only ones around for miles. Yes, the town could produce cider, baked goods, applesauce ..."

Phileas rubbed his chin. "By Jove, you're right. All they need is someplace to make everything. And a delivery system, of course."

Irving smiled. "The millinery could be turned into a bakery."

"Yes, but we should look at it first." Phileas glanced skyward. "We're running out of time, brother." He faced him. "We didn't come here to save the town, just fix a few porches and do a little painting."

"A little?" He laughed. "What about the hotel?"

Phileas stood proudly. "I'm an artist. That's different."

"Ha. Not so much. Face it, we're growing attached to this place."

Phileas smiled. "Are you sure it's just the place?"

Another chill went up Irving's spine, and Sarah flashed before him once more. "I'm sure."

Phileas said no more and started walking again.

Irving sighed and followed. He didn't want Phileas thinking he wouldn't do his duty. He was the most logical choice to take care of business. And though there was a small chance Sterling would still go home, he wasn't going to count on it. He'd set his mind on doing what he had to as his father's second son.

When they reached Sarah's, Flint and Lacey were already working on the fence. "Mr. Darling!" Lacey cried. She dropped her brush and ran to him. "Look what I'm doing!"

"Whitewashing," he said. "And doing a good job?"

She nodded and ran back to her brush. Miss Parsnip and Mrs. Winkle sat in the grass as if watching her.

Phileas took in the scene and smiled. "What good workers."

"They are. And eager to help." Irving went to inspect the fence. "Excellent job, you two."

Flint gave him a half-hearted smile. "It's kinda boring."

"Well, if you think whitewashing is boring," Irving said, "what will you do when we paint the inside of the house?"

"Painting is more fun." Flint looked at him. "For one, you get to use a ladder."

Phileas' face screwed up. "How does that make it fun?"

"I like being up high." Flint looked him over. "Is he all you've brought?"

Irving laughed. "For today. He's going to help me paint."

"But I want to help," Flint said with a frown.

"Don't worry, you'll do your fair share." He bent to Lacey. "Well, look at you – hardly a mess in sight."

"Thank you. Mrs. Winkle has been telling me what to do." She looked at her dolls. "Haven't you?"

Phileas smiled. "Such an adorable work force. Irving, how are you holding up?"

He straightened. "What an odd question."

"Is it?" Phileas looked around. "The house needs painting."

"Yes. Come, I'll show you the inside." He headed for the porch.

Phileas followed. "Where is the Widow Crawford?"

He stopped when they reached the front door. "In the back, doing laundry."

"Hmm."

They went inside, and Irving waved at their surroundings. "The parlor."

Phileas cringed. "Oh dear. This is far worse than Cassie's place."

"Indeed. Follow me." He went into the next room. "The kitchen."

Phileas' eyes widened. "That's it?"

"And two bedrooms." He went to Sarah's bedroom door, knocked, then opened it.

Phileas stepped inside. "Egad, what's that smell?"

Irving smiled. "A family of skunks living under the house." He stepped back into the kitchen and looked out the window. Sarah was hard at work. "Come, let's say hello to Sarah."

Phileas smiled and nodded. "This ought to be interesting."

Irving went to the door and stopped. What did he mean by that? He rolled his eyes. He didn't want to think about it. He was more concerned with keeping himself from falling in love.

Sarah stopped scrubbing at the sound of the back door. Her heart leaped in her chest before she saw Irving, and when she finally did, it melted. She'd dreamed about Irving Darling all night. In her dreams, they did nothing out of the ordinary. They were talking, laughing, much as they'd done over the last couple of days. Maybe that was all there was, but it was enough. She was falling for him and didn't know how to stop from crashing into heartache and misery after he was gone.

"Sarah," he said softly. "How are you this morning?"

She watched him come down the porch steps. One of his brothers was with him. Phileas? Yes, that was him, the one that liked to paint. Was that why he was here? "Hello."

Irving smiled as he approached. "Hard at work I see." He studied the washtub, then looked into her eyes. "How are you feeling?"

She glanced at Phileas and back. "Fine." She swallowed hard. "You?"

"Wonderful."

They stood and stared at each other. She wanted to look away but couldn't.

"Well, now isn't this something?" Phileas drawled. "So nice to see you again, Mrs. Crawford." He crossed his arms and glanced between them. "That is, Sarah. We've, um ..." He peered at them more closely. "... brought some paint." He smiled and waved a hand in front of Irving's face.

He snapped to attention. "Yes, paint."

Her cheeks heated. Goodness! They'd locked gazes and neither looked away. Did that mean ... no, how could he have feelings for her? She wiped her hands on her apron then rubbed her face. Did she have dirt on it? Is that why he was staring at her? But if he was looking into her eyes, how could he see what was on her face?

"We have some samples," Phileas said and studied her wash area. "Care to take a look?"

"You've yet to see the children's room," Irving said.

"What?" Sarah wiped her face again. "You've shown him the house?"

"I have." He took her elbow and steered her toward the porch. "We can get started on the painting."

"Oh, my, that was fast." She shouldn't act so surprised. He'd already told her about the painting. Problem was, every time he was around, she got flustered in the worst way. Her heart pounded, she couldn't take her eyes off him, and when he spoke her insides melted. It was embarrassing. She wasn't some silly calf-eyed schoolgirl, she was a grown woman. A lonely, forlorn grown woman, but still.

Inside, the men looked around the kitchen. "Yellow or green?" Phileas said. "With some lovely curtains." He fingered the torn one in the window over the dry sink. "My, my."

Sarah hung her head in shame. She kept meaning to buy fabric and make new ones but never had enough money. She even thought of tearing her work dress apart to make some out of the skirt, but she had so few clothes, it wasn't a viable option.

"Which would you like?" Irving asked, gently.

She looked at him, noticed how close he stood next to her, and almost fell over. "I ... I'm not sure. You pick."

Phileas went to the center of the kitchen. "The light green, with gingham curtains, red and white, I think. And a lovely tablecloth, of course."

"Tablecloth?" She looked at her sad table with its slight sag in the middle. She could do with a new one but that wasn't happening anytime soon.

"Don't worry about it right now," Irving soothed.

She drew in a breath. He noticed her apprehension? Oh, dear.

"Fine, let's try the green." Phileas marched out of the kitchen.

"Where is he going?" she asked.

"To fetch the paint. We left it outside." He smiled at her. "The fence looks nice."

"Are they covered in whitewash?"

"The fence posts or the children?"

She cracked a smile. "The children, of course."

"No."

"It's a miracle." She laughed. "Especially for Lacey."

"They're fine. Mrs. Winkle is keeping Lacey in line." He put his hand on her shoulder. "They'll do a good job."

Her heart stopped and her breath caught. "Good."

He placed his free hand on her other shoulder. "The place is going to look great." His eyes roamed her face and settled on her lips.

"Yes," she whispered. "Great."

"I know we said green, but I still brought ..." Phileas stopped. "Um, the yellow."

Irving stepped back and cleared his throat. "Yes, yellow." He smiled at Sarah. "For your room?"

Her hand to her chest, she stared at him, then Phileas, who wore a silly grin. "Erm, yellow. Yes. That would be nice. You painted Cassie's bedroom yellow, didn't you?"

"Her sewing room," Phileas corrected with a smile. His eyes skipped between them, and he chuckled. "I'll find a little spot to test the paint."

Sarah went crimson. Good grief, what did Phileas think?

Irving cleared his throat again. "Yes, jolly good, brother." He joined him at the worktable as Phileas pried open the can.

Sarah watched the two, her heart breaking. She had

only so much time left with Irving. Should she enjoy it or avoid him? And after he left for England, what was she to do? Should she break her back continuing to do laundry or seek something better like he said? What would it hurt to look at the old millinery?

She licked dry lips, a hand to her belly, then glanced out the window at the piles of laundry. "I should get back to work."

"See how the paint looks first," Irving suggested. "If you like the shade, then we'll return to town and purchase enough to do the whole kitchen."

She nodded but said nothing – she didn't dare open her mouth, so many things were racing through her head. Like how handsome she found Irving, how generous and kind. He was the type of man to grow old with, to live out her days at his side and be what he needed when he needed it. And he would do the same for her. He already was.

"Sarah?" he said softly.

She shook herself. "Huh?"

"The paint?" He nodded at the wall by the kitchen table.

"Oh." She went to stand next to Phileas, who still held the brush in his hand.

"What do you think?" he asked. "Too light?"

"No, it's just right." She swallowed hard, wrung her hands a few times, then headed for the back door. "Do the whole kitchen." She hurried out the door to the washtub, her heart in her throat. A tear fell, then another.

She had no business falling in love, but here she was. Drat it all! What was she going to do now?

She gripped the edge of the washtub and stared into the soapy water. "Why, Lord? Why him? He's leaving. Leaving!" She wiped at her eyes and drew in a deep breath. There was no use lamenting to the Almighty about it. She was the one that didn't guard her heart well. Now look what had happened!

Sarah squared her shoulders and got back to work. She'd let them paint, fix the floor in her room, and as soon as the house was done, be rid of Irving Darling. The sooner the better. In fact, she'd avoid him from here on out. It was all she could think of. How else could she protect herself from a broken heart?

Chapter Fourteen

Phileas started painting the kitchen as Irving helped the children finish the fence. By the time they were done with that, it was almost time for lunch. Irving went to the back of the house to check on Sarah, who was hanging laundry on the line. "Do you need any help?"

"No."

Irving studied her a moment. She seemed stiff, stand-offish. "Are you sure?" He looked at the rinse tub. "Have you finished?"

She hung up a pair of trousers. "Yes."

He studied her some more. "Is there ... something the matter?"

"No."

His hands went to his hips. "My dear woman, all I've got out of you is yes or no. Can I at least get a maybe?"

She bent to get another pair of trousers and stopped.

"*Maybe* you could help me hang these clothes." She straightened. "Or if you prefer, hang all of them while I start lunch."

Irving smiled. "I can do that."

She went to move past him, but he caught her arm. "What are you doing?" she asked.

"Sarah, if something's wrong you'd tell me, wouldn't you?"

"I don't know. It's not as if ..." She looked away. "Never mind." She pulled her arm from his hand and headed for the house.

Irving watched her go. "Was it something I said?" He stood and puzzled a moment, then started hanging laundry. When he was done, he went into the house to find Sarah at the worktable making sandwiches. Phileas was painting the other side of the kitchen. "I'll open the windows in the parlor, shall I?"

"And the door," Phileas said. "This house is so small; I'm afraid the whole place will smell like paint." He looked sheepishly at Sarah. "Terribly sorry about that."

She shrugged. "It can't be helped."

Irving took one last look at her then went to open the front door and some windows. The children, now in their room, were playing. He'd open their windows too.

When the task was done, he returned to the kitchen. Sarah stood at the worktable staring at a platter of sandwiches. "We should eat these outside," she said.

"Phileas," Irving said. "Put that brush down and help me with the table, will you?"

Phileas set the brush on top of the paint can then went to help him. Once they had the table and chairs moved outside, Sarah brought the sandwiches out.

"We're eating in the backyard?" Flint asked as he came down the porch steps. "This will be fun!"

Lacey followed behind him. "Where am I going to put Miss Parsnip and Mrs. Winkle?"

Irving smiled. The dolls usually leaned against the windowsill at one end of the table. "They could sit in the grass and watch us eat."

"Where?" Lacey looked around.

"At the base of this tree." Irving pointed to the tree one end of the clothesline was tied around. "They'll have a lovely view from there."

Lacey skipped to the tree, set her dolls down and told them to behave. Irving smiled as she skipped back to the table and sat. "What's for lunch?"

"They look like ham sandwiches to me," Irving said.

Phileas joined him. "There are only four chairs. I'll sit on the porch steps."

"You don't mind?" Irving asked. The way Sarah was acting, maybe he should sit there. It was as if she didn't want to be around him.

"All the better to observe." Phileas waggled his eyebrows, grabbed a napkin and a sandwich, and headed for the back porch. He waited for Sarah to come down the steps, then planted himself.

She brought a pitcher of lemonade to the table and

set it down. "What are you doing over there?" she asked Phileas.

"I'm about to partake of this wonderful lunch you prepared. And there are only four chairs." He gave her a silly grin.

She laughed. "Very well." She sat at the table, said a quick blessing, then gave Flint and Lacey each a sandwich.

Irving watched her and took one for himself. "As soon as the kitchen's done, we can do the parlor."

She nodded but said nothing.

"Phileas and I will have to take the furniture outside of course."

Again, she nodded.

"Though if you'd like, we could take a peek at the millinery shop."

She stopped chewing and looked at him. "What?"

"There's one thing you should know about my brother. He loves to paint. While Phileas is doing that, we could see what the millinery has to offer. What do you think?" He took a bite of sandwich and waited.

She stared at him a moment, wide-eyed. "Together? Oh, dear."

He swallowed. "Isn't that what we planned?"

"Well, yes, but ..."

"If you don't wish to, just say so." He took another bite. What was wrong with her today?

"Yes, fine." She stared at her food a moment. "Flint, Lacey, be sure you eat everything."

"Shall we take them with us?" Irving asked. "I'm not sure how much painting Phileas will get done if we leave them behind."

She sighed. "Of course we'll take them."

He glanced at the children. "Sarah," he said quietly. "What aren't you telling me?"

She sat, ramrod straight. "What makes you think I'm not telling you something?"

"You're certainly not yourself," he said. "What else am I to think?"

She blinked a few times then began to look around.

So, evasive maneuvers, was it? He put down his sandwich. "If you're nervous about the house, moving, any of it, then tell me now."

"Of course, I'm nervous. For crying out loud, Irving, in case you haven't noticed, I'm always nervous." She drummed her fingers on her sandwich, noticed what she was doing and stopped. "See what I mean?"

He gaped at her. "My word. Whatever is the matter?"

"Well, if you don't know ..." She bit her lower lip. "Forget I said anything. Yes, we'll look at the millinery shop and get it over with." She left her chair, picked up her plate and grabbed the children's.

"Hey," Flint said. "I'm not done yet."

She took the last of his sandwich and handed it to him. "Finish, then."

Irving watched her march toward the house. Phileas, seeing her coming, vacated his spot just before she reached the porch steps and went inside. He shrugged at Irving. "What the devil?"

Irving shrugged back. "Women."

"Indeed." Phileas joined him at the table. "Seems she's in a bit of a snit today."

"Quite," Irving said. "Though I can't understand why."

"I think she's tired," Flint said. "She gets cranky when she's tired."

"That makes sense," Irving said. "One more reason to see the millinery shop."

"Mr. Darling?" Lacey said. "If Mama lives in the hat shop, do we get to live there too?"

He smiled. "Of course, you do, my darling. Why would you not live with your mother?"

She smiled at him. "What did you call me?"

His smile broadened. "My darling?"

"But you're Mr. Darling."

"Well, one is a name, the other an endearment."

Her face screwed up in confusion. "What's a dearment?"

Phileas laughed. "So, this is how it is for you, is it? How delightful."

Irving left his chair. "I'm glad one of us is amused."

"Don't get me wrong, brother. They're adorable, both of them."

"Adorable?" Flint said with disgust. "Gee whiz, I don't want to be adorable."

"You're quite right," Irving said. "Adorable isn't very manly, is it?"

Phileas laughed. "Lacey's adorable, then."

"And Mrs. Winkle and Miss Parsnip," she tacked on.

"Them too." Phileas looked at the house. "Go to town, see what you can do. This place is too small for this family, or soon will be."

"My thoughts exactly." Irving headed for Lacey's dolls. "Come along, you two. We're going to walk to town."

Lacey jumped out of her chair. "Hooray!"

Irving handed her the dolls. "As your mother seems to be in a mood, we'll do what we can to cheer her up, eh?"

"Maybe she needs a nap," Flint suggested.

"I'm sure she does." Irving looked at the house and crossed his arms. "Poor thing."

"You're making her life easier now, brother," Phileas said. "But what about after we're gone?"

"That's what I'm trying to fix. You don't mind us leaving, do you?"

"I already told you, of course not. Take care of this and you'll rest easier. I hope she will too." He headed for the house. "Time I got back to painting."

"All right, children," Irving said. "Let's fetch your mother."

Flint and Lacey raced for the house and scrambled up the steps past Phileas, beating him inside.

In the kitchen, Sarah was doing the dishes. Irving

smiled at her, took the plate in her hand, and dried it with a rag. "We'll finish these, then go."

"You're so demanding of late." She handed him a cup.

"It's the only way to get things done around here. A man must take charge. Right, Flint?"

"Does that mean I get to take charge of the cookie jar?" he asked.

Sarah rolled her eyes. "Now see what you've done?"

Irving grinned, then nodded at Flint. "Go fetch the cookie jar."

The boy ran into the larder, brought back the jar, and set it on the worktable. "Want one, Mr. Darling?"

"Certainly." Irving set the rag aside and turned to the worktable.

"Not you," Flint said. "The other Mr. Darling."

Phileas joined them. "Don't mind if I do. Have a lovely time in town, all. And see if that millinery shop can't be turned into something."

Irving handed Lacey a cookie, nodded to Phileas, then ushered everyone else out the door.

"You want to do what?" Agnes Featherstone spat.

Sarah squared her shoulders. "We would like to look at the millinery shop. It's still for sale, isn't it?"

"Yes, but you can't afford it." Agnes arched an eyebrow at Irving and the children then glared at Sarah.

"You'll never sell that wreck of a house of yours. And everyone knows you don't have any money."

Sarah glanced nervously around as her cheeks heated. "Be that as it may, we'd like to look at it."

Agnes looked at Irving. "She's not swindling *you* out of any money, is she?"

He glared at her. "No. It was my suggestion that she come look. I think the shop would do her well."

Agnes' eyes narrowed. "Are you buying it for her?"

"What business is it of yours? Are you going to give us the key or not?"

Sarah caught the sternness in his voice and hoped Agnes didn't push him further. Thankfully, before she could open her mouth again, Mr. Featherstone came out of his office. "Agnes, what's going on out here? What's all the fuss about?"

She pointed an accusing finger at Sarah. "*She* wants to look at the millinery shop."

Mr. Featherstone's eyebrows shot up. "Really? But Mrs. Crawford, you could hardly afford it." He noticed Irving next to her. "Mr. Darling, what a pleasure. Are you two looking at it together?"

"We are," Irving stated. "Kindly tell your wife to give us the key."

"Agnes, what's the matter with you?" Mr. Featherstone scolded. "Give Mr. Darling the key and let them look."

"But Francis, it's a waste of time. She can't afford it." Agnes crossed her arms and scowled.

"I'll be the judge of that." He opened the top drawer of Agnes' desk, pulled out a key and handed it to Irving. "I'd take you myself, but I don't have the time. Agnes?"

"Certainly not. I'm not wasting my time either." She shuffled some papers on her desk, picked up a pen and dipped it into an inkwell. "Don't just stand there – take a look, then bring back the key."

Sarah sighed in relief. "Thank you, Mr. Featherstone. We'll be back momentarily." She turned on her heel and headed for the bank doors. Agnes was an infuriating woman who never let her forget how poor she and Caleb were. After he passed, she went out of her way to tell everyone how bad things had become. Of course, things were bad, but Agnes didn't have to announce it to the town every chance she got.

"Horrible woman," Irving said when they were outside. "I don't know how Mr. Featherstone puts up with her."

"No one does," Sarah said. "But Mr. Featherstone has always been a gentle soul, not to mention a bit ... how shall I put it, confused at times?"

"I've haven't noticed. I've not had many dealings with the man."

She took Lacey's hand and headed next door to the millinery shop.

When they reached the building, they looked at the large display windows on the first floor, then at the second story. "I don't know what to expect."

Irving smiled. "Keep an open mind, in case the place isn't well-kept."

"What does that matter? If it's not, one cleans it up." She stared at the doorknob. "Go ahead, unlock it."

Irving smiled at her and opened the door.

Sarah took a breath and stepped inside. "Goodness, this is larger than I expected." There were long counters on either side of the shop with shelves behind both.

"Plenty of room, that's for certain." Irving studied the space.

Flint and Lacey raced for the back. "What's behind this curtain?" Flint asked.

Sarah headed that way. The purple velvet curtains probably led to the work area where Mrs. O'Halloran used to make her hats. She pushed the curtains to one side and smiled. "Look at all this room."

"Where do the stairs go, Mama?" Lacey headed for the staircase at the far wall.

"They must go up to the living quarters." Sarah looked around. There was a long worktable, and several smaller ones.

"This could be made into a large kitchen," Irving said behind her.

She jumped, her hand to her chest. "Goodness!"

Irving smiled. "I'm sorry, I didn't mean to startle you." He took off his hat and looked into her eyes. "There's a lot you can do with this, Sarah. You should consider purchasing."

"It's a little overwhelming," she confessed. "In fact, I wouldn't know where to begin."

"Well, first you'd need to decide what you would use it for, based on what you love to do. I know it's not laundry." He winked.

"Certainly not."

"Mama," Lacey called from halfway up the staircase. "Let's see what's up here."

She sighed. "Here we go."

They joined the children and went upstairs to a landing. Irving opened the door and stepped inside. "My, look at this."

Sarah gasped. The first room was a large parlor, and beyond that the dining room. A door just inside the dining room on the left must lead to the kitchen. Two sets of windows graced the dining room's right wall, the same with the parlor. She noticed another door at the back of the parlor. "Where does this lead?" She opened it and stepped inside. "My goodness."

Irving followed her. "What a large bedroom. And look," he said and pointed. "The windows overlook the orchard."

She went to them and looked out. "What a lovely view."

"Let's see what else this place has to offer." Irving headed for the door. They went into the dining room, through the door on the far wall and into another bedroom. "This one overlooks the street."

Lacey ran inside. "Mama! There's a bathroom!" She grabbed Sarah's hand. "Come see."

Sarah let her drag her out of the front bedroom, through the kitchen and into a tiny hallway that led to another room. "This could be a third bedroom." She looked around. "Where's Flint?"

"In the bathroom," Lacey said with a roll of her eyes. "Come see." She pulled her out of the bedroom and through the other door. "See?"

Sarah gaped at the tub, sink and, blessed be, a commode. "My goodness. I've never seen anything so beautiful."

Irving came into the room and looked around. "The question is, is there hot water?"

"I believe there is. Oh, Irving." She spun to face him. "It's lovely. There's so much space!"

"This is like three of our houses, Mama," Lacey said. "Can we live here?"

Sarah had to still her racing heart. She could never afford it. Never. "We shouldn't have come. This is a mistake."

Irving took her hand and held it. "No, you had to see it. And if you get a good price for your place, you can afford this. But you must decide what you want to do. Do you want to bake? Mend clothes? Make and sell them? If the O'Hallorans could make a living doing it, so can you."

"Yes, but ... Mrs. O'Halloran was a much better

seamstress than I. Of course she was able to sell what she made."

"Then speak to Jean about sharing the space downstairs. The two of you could bake, sew, do any number of things."

"But to do that we'd have to convert part of the work area to a kitchen."

"I'll speak to the captain. I'm sure he knows someone in Virginia City or even Bozeman that can easily do the work."

Sarah's free hand went to her chest. "I don't know ..."

Irving took and held that hand too. "Sarah, sweetheart, don't be afraid. I know it's new, and I know it's scary, but you can do this. I know you can."

She looked into his eyes. He sounded so sure of her. If only she felt the same. "What if I fail?" There it was, her worst fear.

He closed his eyes a moment, then looked at her. "You won't."

She tried to pull her hands from his, but he wouldn't let go. "There are no guarantees ... and Agnes, she'd snatch this place out from under us so fast ..."

"I'll handle Agnes," he said. "You leave that woman to me."

"Oh, Irving, what are you getting me into?"

Without warning he pulled her into his arms. "Nothing I can't handle." He closed his eyes and held her close, as if he could give her some of his strength.

She should step away but couldn't manage it. He was so strong, so warm, and the feel of his arms around her gave her a sense of safety she'd never had before. If she thought she was in love before, she was a goner now.

A giggle caught her attention, and she opened her eyes. When had she closed them?

"What are you doing?" Lacey asked.

"Giving your mother some courage," Irving said. He let go and stepped back. "Say the word, and I'll take care of everything."

She gaped at him. "What?"

He took her by the arms. "Sarah, you heard me. Say the word, and I'll take care of this for you. The sale of your house, the purchase of this place, you need only think about what you want to do with it. I don't want you to fret." He brushed a wisp of hair from her face, his fingers gently caressing her cheek.

A shiver went up her spine, and her knees went weak. "I ... don't understand."

"You need someone to take care of you." He turned away. "Dash it all."

"Irving? What are you saying?" She noticed Lacey had disappeared.

He glanced around the room too. "I ... that is ... oh, bother!" He closed the distance between them, took Sarah in his arms, and kissed her!

Chapter Fifteen

I rving stepped back, wide-eyed. Great Scott, what did he do that for? Well, other than that he couldn't help himself. "Please, do something."

Sarah stood, her mouth half open, and stared at him in shock. "L-like what?"

"You should slap me." He glanced around the room. Thank goodness the children weren't present. "I apologize. I acted less than a gentleman. You deserve better."

Her face contorted in the oddest way, and she laughed. And laughed some more.

Irving cocked his head. "I say, but is everything all right?" Good grief, his kiss wasn't *that bad,* was it?

She held her hand up, shook her head, but couldn't stop laughing.

"Very well, take a moment." He looked nervously around the room.

Flint raced in. "What's so funny?"

Irving shrugged. "That's what I'd like to know."

Flint shrugged back, spun on his heel and ran out of the room.

Sarah pointed at the door. "We ... should go." She gasped, still trying to regain control.

He hadn't sent her over the edge, had he? "Sarah, I'm so sorry. I don't know what came over ... never mind that, I do. The point is I ..."

She waved him to silence. "Stop. Please." A tear trickled down her cheek, and she quickly wiped it away.

He nodded, afraid to say anything else. She was upset but trying to cover with laughter. What a fool he was. He'd had no business kissing her. And though it was just a peck, for him it was so much more.

They returned to the parlor where Sarah stared at the door leading to the landing. "This place. It's so big."

"Plenty of room for a growing family," he pointed out.

"Growing children, you mean." She crossed to the windows and looked outside. "You can see the bank from here. And the sheriff's office."

"Good views all around." He twisted his hat in his hands. She hadn't slapped or screamed at him, only laughed. It was unsettling, really.

"I do like it," she stated. "But I can't afford it." She turned around and looked at him. "Thank you for showing it to me, Irving. But I don't see how I can make it work." With that she headed for the door. "Children!"

Flint and Lacey raced out of the kitchen. "Yes, Mama? Are we going to live here now?"

"No. We just came to look. It was something fun to do, wasn't it?"

Irving heard the quaver in her voice and his heart sank. "Poor poppets," he said softly.

"What?" Sarah said.

He shook his head at her. "Nothing. We'll go if that's what you'd like."

"It is." She went through the door and headed downstairs, the children following.

Irving took one last look around, then closed the door behind him. Downstairs he studied the work area, then the storefront, and noticed Sarah and the children were already outside. "Blast." Leave it to him to make a mess of things. But how to fix it?

He joined them and headed back to the bank. Sarah didn't say much as the children kept asking about the shop. She gave them clipped one-word answers.

Lacey decided to ask him instead. "Mr. Darling, do we get to live there? I like it. There's lots of room. But what would we do downstairs? Do we live there too?"

"Hmmm, I'm afraid I can't answer you, poppet. Your mother isn't as enthused about the place as you and your brother are."

"But why not?" She looked at him with those big blue eyes.

"Because I made a mistake. I thought it was something obtainable but it's not. I'm so sorry."

Lacey stopped. "So am I." She hugged her dolls and hung her head.

The sight tore Irving's heart out, but there was nothing he could do. Sarah wasn't willing to take the risk, and if she had been, he'd just ruined it by kissing her. What a dolt.

When they reached the bank Sarah and the children waited outside while he returned the key. "Back so soon?" Mr. Featherstone asked. "What did you think?"

Irving sighed. "I think it would do quite well as a facility for producing certain things."

Mr. Featherstone's eyebrows shot to the ceiling. "Excuse me?"

"Forgive me, I'm gibbering. I'm afraid Mrs. Crawford doesn't think it will suit."

Mr. Featherstone's face fell. "Oh, that's too bad. I think she could do a lot with that place, so long as she could afford it."

"So do I. However, your wife didn't help when we came for the key."

Mr. Featherstone's ears went pink. "I apologize for Agnes' behavior. Ever since you and your brothers came to town, she's been worrying herself to death."

"That's what you call worrying?" Irving said. "Badgering and belittling the townspeople?"

He shrugged. "Unfortunately for Agnes, that's how she worries. She takes it out on everyone else. Most folks just steer clear of her, but you were an easy target."

"I see." Irving put on his hat. "Thank you for taking

the time, Mr. Featherstone. Perhaps we'll speak again." Without waiting for an answer, he left the bank and rejoined Sarah and the children. "Is there anything you need from Alma's?"

"No, thank you," she said, looking straight ahead. "You've done quite enough for us already. I can't take any more of your charity."

She was being straightforward, with a hint of icy indifference. "I understand. Let's be off, then."

Flint and Lacey ran ahead, then started skipping. Sarah didn't say a word. Irving didn't either, because at this point there wasn't much else to say. He'd already apologized for kissing her and said what he could about the shop. Obviously, she'd made up her mind and wasn't even going to try. Blasted kiss.

By the time they reached her house, Phileas was almost done with the kitchen. "Great Scott, brother," Irving said when he walked in. "You've outdone yourself."

"I've just the ceiling and a bit behind the stove. It's a small room, Irving. It went quickly." He glanced at Sarah and smiled. "How was town?"

"Educational." She brushed past him to the back door.

They watched her go outside. "Is it just me," Phileas said, "or is she in a worse mood than before?"

"She is." Irving went to the stove, checked the coffee pot, then went to the hutch that now stood in the middle of the kitchen. "It's my fault."

Phileas let go an exasperated sigh. "What did you do?"

Irving poured himself a cup of coffee. "I kissed her."

Phileas took one look at him and laughed. He then looked around, obviously making sure they were alone. "And?"

"She laughed." He sipped the bitter brew, made a face, then retrieved the sugar bowl from the cupboard in the hutch. "It wasn't much of a kiss, really. I barely brushed my lips against hers. But to laugh at me ..."

Phileas went to the back door and looked out the window. "She looks angry."

"Oh, trust me, brother, she is." Irving stirred sugar into his cup. "She liked the place. Loved it, even. Then I had to go and do something stupid."

Phileas grinned like a loon. "You and Conrad. Poor chaps. You're as lost as he was at this point."

Irving's eyebrows shot up. "Excuse me?"

Phileas nodded, still wearing the same silly grin. "Face it, brother, you're in love."

Irving's jaw dropped.

"Very in love." Phileas grabbed a cup and poured himself some coffee. Irving was still staring at him, dumbstruck, as he stirred in cream and sugar. "It was bound to happen. You've been spending day in and day out with the woman and her children. They're an adorable little family. I can't blame you." He took a sip of coffee, then grinned again.

"And what about you?" Irving retorted. "You've been spending a lot of time with Dora."

"No, I've been spending a lot of time with Sterling, then Conrad, and now you." He took another sip.

"Dash it all, man. Fine, you're right." He closed the distance between them and lowered his voice. "I'm in love. Happy?" He pointed at the kitchen door. "But she obviously isn't, or she wouldn't have laughed at me when I kissed her."

"Brother," Phileas said calmly, "did it ever occur to you that the poor woman was in shock?"

"From a kiss?" Irving scoffed.

"Of course. Especially if she has feelings for you. But perhaps she doesn't think you have any for her, and then you kiss her. She can't believe it, so she laughs." He took another sip of coffee. "Shock."

Irving's jaw went slack, and he looked at the back door. "By Jove, you might be right." He replayed the kiss in his mind. He did take her by surprise, which was one of the reasons he didn't want to give her a real kiss. Just a simple brush of the lips. It took all his restraint, but he managed it. "She didn't slap me ..."

Phileas laughed. "I rest my case. Perhaps I should become a barrister. I'm rather good at this."

He spun to him. "But she hasn't said anything. Given no indication ..."

"Of course not, you dolt. We're leaving." Phileas arched an eyebrow. "At least some of us are. What about you?"

Irving rubbed his face. "I don't know anymore. I can't stay here. The title, estate. I must take care of them."

Phileas set his cup on the hutch. "Irving, you don't know that. Sterling still hasn't made up his mind. I know he might be leaning toward staying, but it's not definite. Besides, if you do stay, there are still three of us that could do the job."

Irving stared at him, bug-eyed. "You ... you mean you'd take over the title and ..."

"If I had to. Of course." Phileas picked up his cup and took another sip.

Irving looked out the back door again, his mind racing. What was he going to do?

A chill went up Sarah's spine as she scrubbed another piece of laundry. She should add more hot water, then realized she hadn't delivered what she washed yesterday yet. "Land sakes. That man has me so flustered I can't think straight."

She let go of the shirt she was washing and fought against tears. Irving's kiss was hard to forget. True, it wasn't a real kiss – in fact, she wasn't sure she could call it a kiss at all. But in that brief peck, Irving managed to send her heart soaring. It soared still, and she didn't know what to do about it. They were alone, the thrill of something new surrounding them, and she was caught up in the magic of it all. Maybe he was too and slipped. It was only natural.

She remembered the first time a similar thing happened between her and Caleb. They were in the root cellar, and she'd gone down for some potatoes. He was reinforcing one of the beams ...

She looked at the entrance to the root cellar. Caleb's kiss was also brief, and, unfortunately, nothing like Irving's.

She got back to scrubbing. This was far worse than she'd thought. If he had any true feelings for her, that kiss would have been so much more. But as it was, the little peck was a last-minute decision on Irving's part.

She tried not to think about it and continued washing clothes, despite the cold water. As soon as she had this batch hanging on the line, she'd return to town and make her deliveries. The only one who would fuss was Agnes and that was too bad.

Sarah tried to hum, and time her scrubbing to the tune. She was doing everything she could not to think of Irving. She should've slapped him but couldn't. She'd wanted him to kiss her.

She put the back of her hand to her mouth to stifle a sob. This was ridiculous! Yet her heart was breaking all the same. "You fool. You stupid, silly fool." She brushed away a tear, then another. The men were still inside, and she didn't want either of them to see her like this. She'd bury herself in work, let them do theirs, and soon they'd be out of her hair. Then she would never see Irving Darling again.

She finished the washing, did the rinsing, and hung the clothes to dry. This batch would take a while. She couldn't wring the water out as well as Irving could.

By the time she slipped into the house, Phileas had finished the kitchen. "Oh, my," she whispered. The light green was lovely, and she could see his vision for red and white checkered curtains and a matching tablecloth. One day, when she had the money, she'd make them.

She went into the parlor, noticed half the furniture missing, then went onto the front porch. Flint, Irving, and Phileas had already removed the sofa, two chairs, and were heading back inside for the rest. "Can you get the parlor done today?" she asked Phileas as he passed.

"At least half. I hope you don't mind if your furniture is outside overnight. We can put it on the porch."

"Thank you. I wouldn't want a raccoon trying to make a home in my sofa." Flint marched past, a determined look on his face. "Where are you going, son?"

"To get more furniture, what else?" He went into the house.

Sarah smiled as tears stung her eyes. He was trying so hard to be grown-up.

"He worked well today," Irving commented beside her.

Sarah refused to look at him, but that didn't stop her from shivering. "I don't want him to grow up too soon, but I know he has to."

Irving chuckled. "He's only six, Sarah. He won't grow up overnight."

"I know. But the thought still scares me."

He turned her to face him. "I understand. I ... hope I don't scare you. I didn't mean to earlier and I do apologize."

She looked into his eyes. "You're asking my forgiveness, aren't you?"

"I am. Do I have it?"

She swallowed hard and nodded. "Yes. I forgive you, Irving." She shrugged. "You were just stealing a kiss." That said, she hurried into the house.

Wouldn't you know, he followed. "Sarah ..."

She spun around to face him. "Let's not talk about it anymore. It's past." She looked at the floor. "You'll do your work, then leave."

He tucked a finger under her chin and lifted her face to his. "Are you sure about that?"

She frowned. "You've been saying it often enough. Now if you'll excuse me, I have work to do." She left the room and hurried out the back door.

Thank heaven he didn't follow this time. She stopped at the washtub and rolled her eyes at her own stupidity. "Land sakes, of course he didn't. He came back into the house to get more furniture." He had no feelings for her, he was just trying to get the work done.

She looked at the house. Part of her wanted him to come outside. But he didn't. She sighed, spied the clothesline, and realized her washing was done. She went back into the house, brought her baskets of clean, folded laundry outside, put them in the wheelbarrow and set off. As she cut through the front yard, the only one there was Flint, thank goodness. "I'm taking my laundry to town. I'll be back as soon as I can."

"Okay, Ma, I'll look after everything for you."

"Make sure Lacey doesn't get in anyone's way, all right?"

He grabbed her hand, kissed it, then ran for the front porch. "I will!"

Sarah smiled at his retreating form, then left. When she got to town, she headed for the Featherstones' first. It meant passing the millinery shop, and she tried not to look at it as she did. It would only make her think of Irving's kiss, and that was the last thing she wanted right now.

"Sarah," Cassie called from across the street. "Wait."

She watched her cross the street, a happy smile on her face. "What is it?"

"I haven't seen you for a time and wanted to say hello. How are you?"

Sarah took in her happy countenance and smiled. "Apparently not as well as you. You look better than well."

Cassie blushed. "And so I am. Conrad has been ... good for me."

Sarah's heart sank. Irving had been good for her too.

Perhaps too good. "I'm happy for you. You're to be married then?"

"I imagine it's all over town by now." Cassie glanced at the laundry and smiled. "I'll help you deliver this, then I want you to see my house. I know Irving is working on yours. Maybe you'll get some ideas."

She swallowed hard. "Somehow, I doubt that. Not that they didn't do a good job on your place, but my place is so much smaller. Phileas painted the kitchen after lunch and is now doing the parlor."

"He is fast. That's one thing I like about him." Cassie smiled. "He's going to drive Dora plumb loco when he does the hotel."

Sarah smiled. "Has anyone bothered telling Phileas the hotel doesn't belong to him?"

"Someone needs to." Cassie glanced at the wheelbarrow again. "Let's go."

By the time they reached the Featherstones', Agnes was there. Sarah was surprised she didn't complain about not getting her laundry delivered earlier when they fetched the key to the millinery shop.

"About time you got here," Agnes snapped. "Sheriff Cassie. What are you doing with her?"

"Helping with deliveries. Then she's going to have a look at my place."

Agnes sighed impatiently. "Let's get on with it then."

Sarah removed the Featherstones' stack of folded clothes from the wheelbarrow. "Here." She handed them to her.

"You know I need to inspect these," Agnes said.

"Of course. I expect nothing less from you."

Agnes took the clothes and marched into her house. After a few moments she reemerged with some money in her hand. "As usual the ironing is terrible. I'm only giving you half." She shoved the money at her.

Sarah took it, biting her lower lip. "I'm afraid my work is not to your liking. Therefore, I'll no longer be washing for you."

Agnes' eyes popped wide. "What? I haven't dismissed you. You'll continue to wash my laundry for me. If you ever learned to iron, I'll pay full price of course."

"Why doesn't Sarah just wash the clothes and let you iron, Agnes?" Cassie suggested. "Then you'll have them ironed perfectly every time."

Agnes' jaw dropped. "What? Me, iron? Never." She stepped inside and slammed the door.

Sarah blew out a breath. "That woman."

"You don't have to do her laundry, you know. She's just trying to bully her way into not having to pay you for the work."

Sarah bit her lip again as tears welled up. "I know."

"Hey," Cassie said gently as the first tear fell. "What's wrong?"

Sarah gulped a breath and wiped the tear away. "Nothing. I'm ... just tired."

"No wonder, having to put up with the likes of Agnes. If it were me, I'd refused to take in her laundry.

But I know you need the money." Cassie took her by the hand. "How are you doing?"

Sarah wanted to pull away but knew how rude it would be. It would also cause Cassie to ask questions. "The children and I are fine." She swallowed hard, picked up the wheelbarrow, and went to make the rest of her deliveries.

Chapter Sixteen

Irving caught sight of Sarah as she came up the road pushing the empty wheelbarrow. He and Phileas didn't talk much while she was gone, they were too busy painting. Flint helped by keeping Lacey occupied. They thought it best to let her help when they painted the exterior of the house. And, if she behaved, a small portion of her bedroom.

But before they could do any of that, they had to deal with the unwanted house guests under Sarah's bedroom. "I've never seen a skunk, much less tried to evict a family of them," Phileas said. "How do you think we should proceed?"

"We need to speak to the captain." Irving went onto the front porch as Sarah reached the gate.

"Are you going to tell her?" Phileas asked quietly.

"Tell her what?"

"That you're in love?"

Irving looked at him in alarm. "Don't say a word."

"It's hardly my place, now, is it?" He glanced at Sarah coming through the gate. "But you are going to tell her?"

Irving frowned and shook his head.

"What?!"

"Keep your voice down," he warned. Sarah pushed her wheelbarrow across the yard and headed for the back of the house. "I'll tell her in my good time, and that's only if I decide to stay. There are no guarantees at this point."

Phileas shook his head in amazement. "You foozler. What are you thinking? If you love her, then of course you'll stay. But remember, you can always take her back to England with you."

Irving emitted something between a hiss and a laugh. "Are you mad? Can you imagine the look on Mother's face when I turn up with a wife with two children?"

Phileas smiled. "You said the word."

"What word?"

"Wife."

Irving rolled his eyes. "Stay out of this, Phileas. I'm having a hard enough time as it is."

"Not really. You've hardly had to touch a paintbrush."

"You know what I mean." Irving went into the house and got back to work. They still had another wall to do, then the door trim. Phileas insisted they do the window and doors in white. It would look good and brighten up the place. They decided to paint the parlor the same color as the kitchen, seeing as they had enough paint to cover both rooms.

Lacey wandered out of the bedroom, carrying her dolls. "Mr. Darlings?"

Both men looked at her and smiled. "Yes, pet?" Phileas said.

"Can I paint my room?" She hugged her dolls and smiled at them.

Phileas' eyebrows shot up. "Great Scott, I swear she's using that look like a weapon."

"Her cuteness knows no bounds." Irving bent to eye level with Lacey. "Would you like to paint part of your room?"

She smiled and jumped up and down. "Yes!"

Irving gave Phileas a helpless shrug. "Well, then perhaps we'll let you tackle a wall. But first we need to pick out a color."

She looked at Miss Parsnip. "Yellow!"

"A lovely color to be sure." Irving got to his feet. "But I don't think we'll find a yellow quite as bright as Miss Parsnip's hair."

"The yellow used in Cassie's sewing room is nice."

Both men turned to find Sarah standing a few feet away. "I didn't think you saw Cassie's place," Irving said.

"She showed it to me. I ran into her in town." She crossed her arms as if challenging him to deny it.

"How lovely," Phileas said. "What did you think?"

She smiled. "You outdid yourself. Her place is beautiful. I especially like the wallpaper."

Phileas sighed in satisfaction. "I really have missed my calling. But at least I get to exercise it here." He dipped his brush and got back to work.

"What do you think?" Irving motioned to the freshly painted walls.

"Lovely." She looked at the windows. "Phileas, what do you suggest for curtains?"

"White lace." He smiled at them, then started in on the last wall.

"Would you like to help?" Irving asked.

She uncrossed her arms and rubbed them. "You're doing a fine enough job."

"Are you cold?" he asked with concern.

She looked at him, her eyes misting. "I'm fine." She turned and went into the kitchen.

Irving wanted to follow but didn't dare. Phileas had him thinking, and he wasn't sure what to do. Should he tell her how he felt? Or leave things be, go home and do his duty? He retrieved his brush and got to work. Now he knew why Sterling struggled with his decision. Love did many things to a man, not to mention made him do things. In Sterling's case, it meant giving up the title and estate which were rightfully his as the firstborn son.

But Sterling fell in love with more than Letty Henderson. He'd fallen in love with Apple Blossom itself. The little town and its residents had wormed their way into his brother's heart, and for the life of him, Irving couldn't figure out how. Yes, the place was quaint, charming and all that. But some of its residents were less than cordial. He wondered how long it would be before Agnes drove him "plumb loco," as the locals liked to say.

It didn't take long for them to finish the last wall. "We'll do the ceiling tomorrow," Phileas said. "Then start on the children's room."

"We'd better stop by the captain's and ask him about the skunk problem."

Phileas made a face. "Right." He shuddered. "I hope he doesn't tell us we have to crawl under the house and shoo them out."

"Maybe we could borrow his dog?" Irving suggested.

Phileas looked toward the kitchen. "You should talk to her."

Irving followed his gaze. "We discussed this."

"You owe it to her."

"What?" Irving said. "A detailed explanation on why I kissed her?" He took Phileas' brush from him and headed outside. They'd filled a bucket of water earlier to clean the brushes in.

Phileas came down the porch steps as Irving was dipping brushes into the water. "You know what I meant. At least tell her how you feel."

He shook his head. "There's no point. She doesn't feel the same."

"And how do you know that?" Phileas asked.

Irving stopped swirling the brushes. "She can barely accept what I've done for her so far. She's like a scared rabbit, brother. You honestly think her capable of accepting the way I feel about her?"

Phileas went to the other side of the bucket and got down on one knee. "You won't know until you try."

"And if Sterling stays?"

Phileas shrugged. "Then you take your new love and her adorable children and go home with the rest of us."

"But Mother ..."

"... will get over it," Phileas finished. "You've seen what Lacey can do. Give her two weeks and she'll have Mother and Father eating out of her hand. So will Mrs. Winkle, for that matter."

Irving smiled. He had a point. "I don't think I should rush her."

"Considering our timetable, I don't see any way to avoid it." Phileas got to his feet. "At least tell her. Who knows – if you don't, you might be leaving her behind with a broken heart. And dare I say, she won't be the only one."

Irving tried not to roll his eyes and failed. "All in good time."

"Which we don't have a lot of," Phileas reiterated.

Irving nodded sagely. It was true. He'd have to decide what to do and fast. But so far, Sarah was hard to read, and he didn't relish making a fool of himself in front of her. She was a delicate thing, fragile and frightened. He'd done enough damage as it was.

They cleaned the brushes and set them on one of the old fence posts to dry. "I should be off," Phileas announced. "Are you coming?"

Irving sighed as his chest tightened. He should go, but he didn't want to. Things were still tense between he and Sarah, and he didn't want to leave her in such a state. "I'll be along. You go ahead."

Phileas started for the gate then stopped. "I'll see you at dinner?"

"Yes." His chest tightened further. Why was this so hard?

"Very well, then. I'll tell the others to expect you." Phileas left.

Irving turned to the house and took a good long look at it. If he stayed, could he live in such a dwelling? The garden shed on his family's estate was bigger than Sarah's little house. "What are you getting yourself into, old chap?"

With a sigh, he headed for the porch steps. With any luck, he'd be able to gauge where Sarah's heart was without having to outright ask. If he did ask, he feared he'd frighten her off for good.

Sarah checked each piece of clothing. None were dry yet. No matter, she'd check them again, if only to keep from thinking about Irving. He had a smidge of paint on his cheek, and she wondered if he knew. She noticed a lot of things about him in the few minutes she was in the parlor – the look of concern in his eyes when he met her gaze, the way his head tilted ever so slightly when he was studying her. There was a boyish charm to him, to all the Darlings in fact. Oliver had it in spades.

She smiled and took hold of a pair of Mr. Smythe's denims. Could she live in the millinery shop? Oh, yes. The place was perfect. But how could she afford it? If Agnes had her way, she'd be doing the Featherstones' laundry the rest of her days.

"Here you are."

Her heart jerked at the sound of Irving's voice. "Where else would I be?" She turned around. He stood not feet away, and she wondered how he managed to sneak up on her. "What do you need?"

"Nothing, I just wanted to let you know Phileas and I are leaving." He glanced at the road. "Phileas already left."

She looked toward the road too. "I see. Have you said goodbye to the children yet?"

"No, I'll do that when I'm done here."

She crossed her arms. "And are you?"

He stepped toward her. "Do you want me to be?"

Sarah's heart pounded as her entire body stiffened. "What does that mean?"

He took another step. "When the house is done. Do you ... care to see me anymore?"

Her breath hitched. What was he saying?

"It's just that you've been so out of sorts of late," he went on. "One would think you didn't want me around. If I've done anything to offend you ..." He shrugged helplessly. "... other than kiss you, of course, then I am truly sorry."

So it was back to the kiss, was it? She sighed. "You made a mistake. Men do that sort of thing."

He swallowed. "Kissing?"

"Mm-hmm." She went to the next piece of clothing. Why couldn't he drop the subject? It wasn't even a real kiss.

"Very well, then. I should go." He turned to leave.

"What about the skunks?" She moved away from the clothesline. "What's to be done about them?" She didn't know why she asked, other than to keep him there a while longer.

He twisted his hat in his hands. "Phileas and I were going to speak to the captain."

"If he doesn't have any idea, then talk to Mr. Atkins or Mr. Smythe. They'll know."

"Mr. Atkins did mention something the other day." He slapped his hat against his leg a few times. "I'll pay him a visit."

"See that you do. I don't want my place to stink of skunk for weeks on end."

"Of course not." He put on his hat. "Well, I'm off." He headed for the front yard.

"Thank you," she blurted.

Irving stopped and turned around. "For what?"

"For ... trying to help."

"Trying?"

She shrugged. "The millinery."

He nodded. "I still think it would be good for you and the children."

She hugged herself. "Of course it would, if I could afford it."

"I understand."

Did he? She wondered if he could even conceive what it was like to be poor or know what hunger was. His family were rich farmers. What would they know of poverty?

"Sarah?"

She looked at him and her heart broke. She shouldn't be so hard on him. After all, he was a lovely man that had stepped into her life for a brief time and would be leaving soon. Why couldn't she enjoy the time spent with him and have a few nice memories to keep her company on cold winter nights? "You'd best catch up to your brother."

He nodded. "Goodbye, then."

Her throat grew thick. "Goodbye."

Irving gave her one last parting look, and she thought she might die. His eyes were full of concern, compassion, and the gentleness she'd come to know.

She watched him cross the backyard and disappear around the front corner of the house. It wasn't long before she saw him heading down the road to town.

"Goodbye, Irving." She watched him until the trees blocked her view, then went inside the house.

"Mama," Lacey said as she entered the kitchen. "Where's Mr. Darling?"

"I'm sorry, sweetheart, but he had to go. He meant to say goodbye, but we got to talking, and I'm afraid it's my fault he didn't."

"That's okay," Lacey said. "He'll be back tomorrow. He said I can paint some of my room."

"What?!" Flint called in alarm from the parlor. He raced into the kitchen and came to a skidding stop. "Ma!"

"Whatever your sister does, Flint, can be painted over." She headed for the parlor. "What do you think of their work?" If she talked to the children, maybe it would slow her heart. She was losing her battle with it. What was she going to do when Irving returned tomorrow, and the day after that and the day after that? How many more days of this could she take before her heart broke completely? She heard once that unrequited love was the worst kind. It was true.

She took a shuddering breath and looked over the newly painted walls. Phileas suggested white lace curtains, and she tried to picture them. It wasn't easy. Her mind kept drifting to Irving and the look on his face as he left moments ago.

"Mama, can I have a new dress for the dance?" Lacey asked out of the blue.

Sarah gasped. "What made you ask that? I'm not sure we're going."

"What?" Flint said. "Why not? Everyone else is. Even Billy."

"How would you know?" She closed her eyes and sighed. "Your lessons. Land sakes, I haven't taken you in days."

"That's okay, Mama," Lacey said. "Being with Mr. Darling is more fun."

"Yeah," Flint said. "He doesn't make us do our lessons."

"Well, you'll get them tomorrow," Sarah said. "I've been so busy with the house that I've been lax in your schooling. I'm sorry."

"Don't be." Flint stood, hands on hips. "Real men don't need school."

Sarah facepalmed. "Oh, Flint. Really?"

He grinned and ran out the front door. Lacey followed, giggling all the way.

Sarah let her hand drop, then sighed again. Irving had her more flustered than she'd realized. It was bad enough her heart ached, but his presence had disrupted her children's education. She was surprised Rev. Arnold hadn't sent someone to ask why the children hadn't been in school. Then again, maybe the reverend hadn't been holding classes. He was getting too old to teach or preach. She'd have to make sure they spent time at the captain's tomorrow, regardless.

She looked at the clock on the mantle, surprised

Irving or Phileas hadn't taken that outside too, then went to her bedroom. Once there she sat on the bed, folded her hands in her lap, and took a deep breath. "Oh, Lord, what am I going to do?" Unable to think of anything, she looked at her pillow, fell onto it face first and let herself cry.

Chapter Seventeen

"Are you sure this will work?"

Irving gave Wallis a sidelong glance. "If the captain says it will work, it will."

"Of course, lads," Captain Stanley said. "This method comes from a reliable source."

"I'm not going to ask," Sterling mumbled. He looked at the lemon rinds in his hand. "So the idea is to put these under the house."

"Aye. For whatever reason, skunks hate the smell of lemons and oranges. Should chase them out quick enough." The captain went to Irving, one bushy eyebrow raised in question. "You used the chicken wire?"

"Yes, Flint and I sealed up any openings except this one." He nodded at the back porch.

"Well then, gentlemen, I think we can proceed." The captain, along with everyone else, eyed Oliver.

He rolled his eyes. "Fine, but I don't see why I have to be the one to crawl under there again."

"You're the thinnest, lad," the captain said.

Oliver drew in a breath then exhaled, bracing himself. "Right." He approached the back porch. "Lemons."

The captain handed him a sack of lemon rinds and a small lantern. "Get in, spread the rinds without raising the enemy's suspicion, then get yourself out of there."

Conrad laughed. "You make it sound as if we're at war."

Captain Stanley raised his other eyebrow. "Make no mistake. Those critters will isolate you and ruin your life for weeks if they fire."

"You mean spray, don't you?" Irving asked.

"Same difference." The captain waved Oliver toward the porch. "Get on with it, lad."

Oliver swallowed hard, pulled the kerchief around his neck over his nose and mouth, and crawled under the porch.

Phileas bit a knuckle. Irving took one look and laughed. "Why so nervous?"

"What if he's hit?" Phileas asked. "Poor chap will become an outcast."

"He's right," the captain said. "None of you will want to be around him."

Irving, Sterling, and Wallis bent to peek under the porch.

"Don't," the captain warned. "It's upsetting enough for the little beasts to have Oliver under there."

The three straightened. "I'm with Phileas," Wallis said. "I don't know if I can take the ..."

"Ohhhhhaaaaarrrrrggggghhhhhhh!"

"Oliver!" Phileas cried. "He's been hit!"

The rest of them backed up several paces as Oliver's feet came into view, followed by the rest of him as he shimmied his way out. The awful stink they'd been warned about came with him.

"Oh, gad!" Irving waved his hand in front of his face. "That's terrible. Ollie, are you all right?"

Oliver climbed to his feet, blinking and gagging. A little skunk ran out from beneath the porch and headed for the others. Phileas ran for the nearest tree, Sterling went behind the wash table, and the others sprinted for whatever cover they could find.

Oliver blinked a few more times then looked at them. "One of the little blighters got me!"

Conrad pointed at his feet. "And he's right beside you!"

Oliver looked down. "Blimey!" He ran up the porch steps. The little skunk stomped its feet as another emerged, then another.

"It's working," Sterling said. "They're coming out."

Sarah opened the back door. "What ... oh! Oliver!" She stepped back inside and slammed the door shut.

"That's gratitude for you," he quipped. "I risk my life and for what?"

More skunks waddled out from beneath the porch. "I think you scared the little buggers," Irving said. "Let them be on their way."

"Aye," the captain agreed. "No one move. Let them pass."

A big one came out, making them all cringe. "That must be the mother," Phileas said and ducked behind the tree again.

They watched as six skunks – five babies and their mama – cut across the backyard to the trees and brush beyond. As soon as they were out of sight, the men regrouped a good distance from Oliver. "Oh, dear." Phileas fanned the air in front of him. "This is a problem."

Conrad coughed a few times, then looked at the captain. "How long did you say the smell would last?"

Captain Stanley shook his head in dismay. "Weeks."

Oliver's eyes widened. "Is there no cure?"

The captain gave him a grave look and shook his head again.

"But ... the dance ..." Oliver looked at himself. "My clothes ..." He pulled off his kerchief, then his vest.

"Wait!" The captain held up a hand. "Before you strip, get back under that porch and make sure the little fiends are all gone."

"What?" Oliver pointed to the porch. "You want me to go back down there?"

"You're already done for, lad. Won't hurt you now, will it?"

Oliver looked at his brothers and shrugged. "I suppose not." He stomped down the porch steps, grabbed the lantern he'd dropped after he crawled out, and went back under.

Sarah opened the back door a crack. "Is it safe?"

"More or less," Irving said.

She poked her head out. "Well, are they all gone?"

"The skunks wandered into the brush," Phileas called then came out from behind the tree. "I think that was all of them."

She stepped onto the porch and pinched her nose. "Oh, that's terrible!"

"I'm afraid your house will stink for weeks." Irving shook his head in dismay. "We're sorry, Sarah."

She put her hand over her nose and mouth and looked like she was going to cry.

It was one more thing for her to worry about, and Irving would have none of it. "Don't fret, I'll take care of everything."

Sterling stepped forward. "He means *we'll* take care of everything. This is our fault. Your whole house will be unbearable. Pack some clothes, you're coming back to town with us."

She stared at them. "No, you don't have to ..."

"We want to," Irving cut in. "Pack some things for you and the children. We'll get you a room at the hotel. In the meantime, we'll get the floor done in your bedroom."

She stared at him in panic. "But if I'm at the hotel, how can I do my work?"

"Dora has a place where she washes clothes," Irving said. "She won't mind if you use it. Besides, if you don't have to go back and forth to town, you'll save time."

Her shoulders slumped in defeat. "Very well." She disappeared into the house.

Sterling and the others gathered around Irving. "Poor thing," Wallis said. "She's frightened to death."

"What is she so afraid of?" Conrad asked.

Irving stared at the back door. "Hunger." He turned to his brothers. "Which is why I'll need your help."

Sterling smacked him on the back. "Anything, brother."

Irving smiled and nodded at them. "We've the floor to replace in Sarah's room. Then we'll paint it, finish the children's bedroom, and then take things from there."

"With all of us working, we'll have it done in no time," Sterling said. "Problem is the smell."

"Aye, but you'll be tearing up rotted boards that have been sprayed and can burn them," the captain said. "Once you've laid the new floor it won't be so bad. You can also wheelbarrow in some fresh dirt to help cover the smell before you lay the flooring."

"Good idea." Irving bent to peek under the porch. "Oliver? You all right under there?"

"Yes!" came the muffled reply. "They're gone!" He scooted out from beneath the porch again. "Stinks something awful under there, though."

Everyone grimaced. "So do you, I'm afraid," Phileas said. "Captain, is there anything he can do?"

"Maybe rub himself down with lemons?" He shrugged.

"What about Snow Flakes?" Irving asked. "Aren't they supposed to clean everything?"

"You could try," the captain said. "I know Sarah keeps a box on her windowsill." He eyed the washtub. "She's got a bathing tub she keeps in the shed. I'll fetch it." He headed that way.

Irving started for the porch. "I'll get the Snow Flakes." He went into the house and found Sarah standing next to her closed bedroom door. "Is it that bad?"

She turned around, her eyes red.

"Sarah, have you been crying?" Without thinking he pulled her into his arms. "There's no need to worry. I'll take care of everything."

She stood very still, and he wondered what else could be wrong. He also enjoyed the feel of her in his arms and hugged her close for a moment before letting go. "We'll brave your room together." He opened the door.

She froze.

"Sarah?"

She shook her head. "I don't know what to do ..."

"What?" He went to stand in front of her again. She was staring straight ahead. "Well, I do. You'll pack some clothes for you and the children, then you're ... wait a minute. Where are the children?"

"They're just down the road. There's a tiny brook there where they make mud pies."

"Well, it's best they missed all this. By the way, I need your Snow Flakes for poor Oliver." He cupped her face in his hand, not caring how intimate it was. "I'm taking you and the children to the hotel. My brothers and I will get everything sorted, you'll see."

She looked into his eyes. "Why are you so kind to me?" Her eyes drifted to the floor. "No one but the captain has been this kind."

He brought his other hand to her face. "You deserve kindness." He looked her in the eyes and it was all he could do not to kiss her. But he wasn't going to make that mistake again. He'd rather let his other actions speak for him. "I will take care of this." He let go, stepped back, then went to the dry sink. As soon as he had the box of Snow Flakes in his hand, he hurried out the back door.

Then Wallis went inside. "What is he doing?" Irving asked Sterling.

"He's fetching the kettle to fill and start heating water. The captain already put the bathing tub on the other side of the house. Oliver can wash while we see what we can do with his clothes."

"Burn them?"

Sterling looked at poor Oliver as he began to strip. "That's a good idea. I'll send Wallis to the hotel to fetch him more." He glanced at the house. "Why don't you take Sarah and her children to the hotel while we take care of things here?"

"I am. She's packing now." He headed for Oliver.

"Irving ..."

He stopped and turned around. "Yes?"

Sterling looked him in the eyes. "You care for her."

Irving sighed. There was no use denying it. "Yes."

His brother nodded. "Then you'd best do something about it."

"But the estate ..."

"Isn't going anywhere." Sterling smiled. "We'll handle things."

Irving exhaled. "Then I'd best handle things too."

Sterling winked. "See that you do."

Sarah packed slowly. She couldn't think, didn't want to. It was a silly little skunk, nothing more, but the animal had just turned her world upside down. She didn't want to be dependent on Irving. She didn't want to depend on anyone but herself. Yet she was stuck.

Irving and his brothers were only trying to help, and she'd let Irving do a lot up to this point. But something had changed, and her struggle was reignited. How could she accept his help now? She'd have to deal with the guilt, the shame. Was that it? Was it as he explained before?

"Am I giving up all my control?" She sat on the bed and thought about it. "Pride. Is that what plagues me?" She was young when she became a mail-order bride, barely eighteen. She ran away from her drunken father, half-starved, seeking a better life. Marrying a stranger was the only way she could find to survive. Caleb was a decent man, if unambitious. Then he was gone.

She closed her valise and thought of what to pack for the children. The whole house was beginning to smell as the sour stench of skunk seeped through the cracks between the floorboards. Had several of them sprayed? She didn't know, didn't care at this point. She was going to be stuck in town for a time and wondered if she'd lose any customers because of this. Thank Heaven she'd already delivered her laundry that morning.

Yesterday when she said goodbye to Irving, she'd meant it. She knew she'd never see him again after he finished her house. Now she'd be in the same building with him, would likely be eating meals with him too. How could she keep her heart intact with all that? If she thought she was attached now ...

She went into the children's room and packed up their clothes. Lacey had Mrs. Winkle and Miss Parsnip with her, so she didn't have to worry about the stench permeating her dolls. How horrible would that be?

She took the valises outside and left them by the gate. The smell at the front of the house was just as bad as the back. Poor Oliver. Speaking of which, what was going on in the backyard?

She pulled a handkerchief from her skirt pocket, covered her nose and mouth and walked around the house to see.

"Stop," Irving said with a raised hand as he hurried toward her. "Oliver is ... well, he's removed ..."

"I understand." Her eyes flicked to the pump. "I should heat some water."

"Wallis already filled the kettle and put it on the stove. The captain needs the lemons we peeled. You didn't make lemonade with them yet, did you?"

"No, they're in a bowl in the larder. I was about to when ..." She shrugged. "Poor Oliver."

"Indeed. Wait until Dora finds out. I hope she doesn't make him sleep outside."

"Are there any rooms not in use?"

"Yes, two. I'll get them for you and the children."

Her heart skipped. "One is fine."

"There are only so many beds in a room," he reminded her.

She nodded. It was hard to think around him. It was hard to do anything other than hope and pray she could make it through the next few days. She would never forget him and wondered if she'd ever meet another man like Irving Darling. If only she could be so lucky. "I should fetch the children."

"I'll come with you." He smiled and motioned toward the gate.

She stared at him, unsure what to say. She closed her eyes instead.

"Sarah." His voice was soft, gentle. He wasn't making this easy.

She opened her eyes. "Are you sure Dora has a place I can work?"

He took her hands. "Stop worrying."

She looked at their hands and pulled away. "I'll be back with the children." She turned and headed for the gate. He took the hint and didn't follow. Good. She didn't want to be around him anymore than she had to. This was hard enough. She hoped the lot of them left as soon as they were done with her house, but that wasn't going to happen. She couldn't look a gift horse in the mouth, and needed her floor done now more than ever. She just hoped her house didn't stink like this for too long.

She went up the road, found the children in their usual spot by the brook, and knelt in the grass next to them.

"Hello, Mama," Lacey said happily. "Look at my cookies!" She pointed to a large rock with mud cookies drying in the sun. "Don't they look yummy?"

"They do, sweetheart." Sarah sniffed back a tear.

"Ma, are you okay?" Flint asked.

"I'm afraid Oliver got sprayed by a skunk."

"Ewww!" Lacey said with a grimace. "Does he stink?"

"The whole house does."

Flint's face scrunched up. "Yuck." He suddenly smiled. "I wish I'd been there to see it."

"Flint!" Sarah got to her feet. "Poor Oliver will smell bad for weeks because of this, and our house ... well, Mr.

Darling is having us move into the hotel for a ..." She sighed. "I'm not sure for how long. But I want you two to promise me you'll behave while we're there."

"We will," Flint said, then elbowed Lacey.

"Promise," she said.

"Good. The last thing I need is for you to be running all over the hotel willy-nilly." She headed for the road. "Come along. Mr. Darling is waiting for us."

"But Mrs. Winkle doesn't want to stay in the hotel," Lacey said as she gathered her dolls.

"I'm afraid Mrs. Winkle doesn't have a choice."

"But Ma, who's going to pay for our room?" Flint gave her a questioning look. "Do you have the money?"

Sarah's chest squeezed. "No, Flint. I don't."

"Is Mr. Darling paying for it?" Lacey asked.

She turned away and shut her eyes tight. "He is." When she opened them, they were full of tears. "Don't worry, I'll find a way to repay him." Without turning around, she headed for home. She had lost all control at this point. They were now in Irving Darling's hands.

She didn't want to think about it on the trek back, so instead thought of what else she would need for their stay at the hotel. But her mind kept going back to Irving, his kindness, his way of seeing to their comfort and making sure their needs were met. It also made her think of how she'd isolated herself from those in Apple Blossom. Her pride had kept them hidden away, even from the captain.

How many times had she told Captain Stanley they were doing fine when they weren't? How many times had she gone without food the last three months or so and kept it hidden, even from the children? She was trying so hard to make things stretch that she'd failed to see her children were hungry, even though she was feeding them. What a fool she was.

Well, no more. She'd do what she had to in order to make money, even if it meant leaving Apple Blossom and moving to Virginia City. A bigger population meant more work. If she did sell her place, that's what she'd do. At least she'd go with some funds in her pocket. She could find a small place somewhere, take in laundry as she was doing now. They'd get by with more work, and once Flint was old enough, he could find work ...

She caught sight of Irving waiting at the gate and marched up to him. "How long do you think it will take for the smell to go away?"

"I thought I told you. The captain said weeks." His head tilted to one side. "What's wrong?"

She shook her head. "Nothing. I've just decided to sell the house, that's all." She went through the gate, grabbed the two valises she left there earlier, then went to the middle of the road. "We're off to the hotel."

Irving stared at her a moment, then joined them. "Jolly good." He looked her over again. "Are you sure there's nothing wrong?"

Sarah straightened. "I am. Let's go."

Chapter Eighteen

I rving escorted Sarah and the children into the hotel. Dora was behind the counter and looked up from the book she was reading. "Sarah, what a nice surprise."

He watched out of the corner of his eye as she forced a smile. Why was she so tense? He knew this was inconvenient, but there was nothing else to do but bring them here. "I'm afraid there's been a small ... accident," he explained.

"What?" Dora came around the counter. "What happened?" She looked over Sarah and the children. "Is everyone all right?"

"We're fine," Sarah said. "But my house ..."

"A skunk made our house stink," Lacey said. "Phew!"

Dora's eyes widened. "Oh, I see." She made a face. "Then ... the house got sprayed?"

"Along with Oliver," Irving said. "Terribly sorry. I'm not sure what to do about him."

Dora gaped at him. "And the others?"

"They're fine." He nodded at the counter. "Sarah and the children require two rooms."

"Of course." Dora hurried behind the counter and opened the guest register. "I happen to have a room with two beds. Perfect for Flint and Lacey."

"And Mrs. Winkle and Miss Parsnip?" Lacey held up her dolls.

Dora looked over the counter at her. "Yes, they will be very comfortable. Sarah, I'm giving you the room right across the hall. Oliver ... oh, dear ..."

"He's bathing now," Irving said. "But according to Captain Stanley, it won't do much good."

"He's right. The stench takes forever to lessen, but it will over time." Dora turned the guest register around and pushed it toward Sarah.

"I'll take care of their rooms," Irving said. He noticed Sarah stiffen but said nothing. So that was it. Her pride was getting in the way again.

"That's very kind of you," Dora said. "But under the circumstances, Sarah can have the rooms, no charge."

Sarah stiffened further. Irving sighed. "This is your place of business, and though I know how much Sarah appreciates the gesture, I want to make sure you are paid for the rooms."

Dora nodded and handed Sarah a pen. She took it and stared at the guest register. "I will repay you, Irving."

He put a hand over hers. "No. You won't. There's no need."

She looked at him. "*I* have a need."

His heart sank. Why couldn't she accept his help? She'd been accepting it fine up until now. Well, there were a few bumps, but nothing like this. She seemed angry and put out that he was helping her.

She signed the register, and Dora handed her the keys. "The two rooms at the end of the hall," Dora said. "I'll bring up some fresh towels."

Sarah smiled weakly and nodded. "Come along, children." She headed for the staircase.

Irving gave Dora a nod of thanks and followed them. Upstairs Sarah didn't so much as look at him as she traversed the hall. When they reached the end of it, she went to one of the rooms, tried a key and opened the door. There was a single bed in it. "This is my room." She went inside, placed her valise on the bed, then left the room and crossed the hall. "This one is yours, children." She unlocked the door and ushered them inside. Like before, she set their valise on the bed then turned to him. "Thank you." Her eyes were downcast.

His heart broke. "Is it so bad?"

She met his gaze. "What?"

"My helping you?"

She swallowed. "I am ... in your debt tenfold now."

"You make it sound like a terrible thing." Indeed, he was beginning to wonder if she thought him some cad that would sneak into her room at night and have his way with her as payment for all he'd done.

"I don't like owing anyone for anything." She went to the window and looked out. "Especially now."

"Why now?" He stepped inside the room. "Sarah, what's wrong?" He caught Lacey out of the corner of one eye tucking her dolls in on one of the beds. Flint was at the other window looking out.

Irving joined Sarah. "What have I done?"

She closed her eyes as if in anguish. "Please, just leave."

"Sarah ... I don't understand."

She opened her eyes, looked at him. "You've done too much." She gazed out the window again. "People used to do things for my father, and he squandered their gifts and good deeds. Some didn't take kindly to that."

"But that has nothing to do with me," he said in his defense.

"Perhaps not, but ... I still don't like owing anyone anything."

Irving stood in shock. Was she trying to be rid of him? He sighed. "Very well. I'll leave you to it, then." He turned and left the room.

Downstairs he paced the lobby a few times, drawing Dora's attention. "What's the matter with you?"

He pointed to the staircase. "That is a stubborn woman up there."

Dora smiled. "Oh, yes. Very." She leaned against the counter. "So what'll you do about it?"

Irving pointed at her. "You just wait and see." He strode out the hotel doors. He had a list of things to do, but first things first. He headed straight for the bank.

Sarah saw Irving leave and head up the street. She had no idea where he was going and didn't care. She wanted to be alone, have some time to think. If she was going to put her house up for sale, she'd have to speak to Mr. Featherstone and that could go one of two ways, depending on whether or not Agnes was there. Then again, Agnes might want to be rid of her and tell her husband to find a buyer quickly.

"Children, I'm going for a walk. I'll let Dora know. If there's anything you need, ask her, all right?"

Flint nodded as he stared out the window. Lacey yawned and lay down next to her dolls.

Sarah smiled and left the room. She wouldn't go far. Maybe up and down the street a few times or take a walk through the orchards. Downstairs she informed Dora, then left.

Once outside, she gulped a lungful of air, then headed toward the livery stable and feed store. She knew Irving went in the opposite direction and didn't want to chance running into him. He was the cause of all of this. First, she had to go and fall in love with him. Unrequited love at that. Then she let herself fall deeper and deeper into his debt. She kept having flashes of her father's debtors banging on their door. It scared her half to death. They yelled and called him names and made it sound as if they were going to beat the door down.

Then and there she'd vowed to never owe anyone anything. Was that why it was so hard for her to accept anyone's help? Seemed she could in small amounts, but then she'd get the uncontrollable urge to run and hide. She was having it now.

She sat on a bench outside the sheriff's office. There was no sign of Cassie, which meant she wouldn't have to talk to her. Good.

All she had to do was hold out until the Darlings left, then she could breathe easy. She'd do what she could to repay Irving for at least some of the kindness he'd shown her and the children but wasn't sure how and when. There was just too much to think about right now. Worse, if his brother Sterling stayed, she'd have a constant reminder of Irving, and she wasn't sure she could handle that.

This wasn't the same kind of love she had for Caleb. Yes, she'd loved him, but she wasn't *in* love with him. They got along, were friends even, but there was no ... what was the word? Romance, that was it. He never went out of his way to take her hand or hold her unless it was exceptionally cold. He was just ... there. Sometimes it amazed her they'd had children, but as it was something they both wanted, well, Flint and Lacey were the result.

Now they were fatherless, and she wasn't sure what

to do about that either other than what she was already doing. Little as that was.

She felt like a scared rabbit that couldn't do anything but run from some unseen predator and hope she didn't get caught in a hunter's snare. It was a horrible way to live. In fact, this was how her father had lived. "How did this happen?" She puzzled over it a few more minutes, then left the bench. Irving was across the street, and she didn't want him to see her. She went down the side of the sheriff's office to the apple orchard behind the buildings. She could pick a few and take them back to the children.

Sarah ducked into the trees and hurried down a row. Hopefully Irving hadn't seen her. The sooner he left her alone, the better. Her heart ached enough as it was.

Irving watched Sarah hurry behind the sheriff's office. What was she doing? He looked at the papers in his hand, then headed for the hotel. He didn't see the children with her and figured she'd left them with Dora.

When he reached the lobby, he headed straight for the staircase. "Flint and Lacey upstairs?"

"Yes," Dora said. "I believe Sarah went for a walk."

"Thank you." He took the stairs two at a time. He wanted to put the papers in his room before he spoke with Sarah.

When he was done, he knocked on the children's door. "Flint? It's me, Irving."

Flint opened the door. "Hi. Ma went for a walk."

"Yes, I know. I'm surprised you're not downstairs raiding Dora's cookie jar."

"Nah." He nodded at the bed. Lacey was sound asleep. "I don't want her to wake up alone."

Irving smiled. "You're a good lad to look after your sister. I'll send Dora up with some cookies, how about that?"

He smiled. "Gee, thanks."

Irving's smile grew. "I'll see you after a bit. There's something I need to speak to your mother about." He left and went downstairs to find Sarah. If she didn't accept what he wanted to give her, then what else could he do?

Sarah walked down one row of apple trees, reached the end, then started up the next, eyes fixed on the grassy ground.

A twig snapped and she looked up. "Irving." She sighed. So much for her peaceful walk. He was the last person she wanted to see. She wasn't sure her heart could take it.

"Sarah," he called, jogging toward her.

Tears stung her eyes at the mere sight of him. He was everything she'd ever wanted in a man. It was a crying shame he was so kind, handsome and ...

"There you are." He reached her and smiled. "I

wanted to talk to you, if I may?"

A chill went up her spine, then another. The first was delight, the second dread. She might as well let him have his say. "What is it?"

He looked around, then caught her gaze. "I ... wanted to tell you I'm a fool."

Her eyes widened. That got her attention. "Excuse me?"

"Everyone's been telling me to speak to you, but I admit, I thought you'd be ... uncomfortable with the conversation."

"Conversation? This isn't about our kiss again, is it?"

"No, of course not." He took her hands in his. "It's about you."

"Me?" She wanted to pull away, but his hands were so large, warm and comforting, she couldn't bring herself to. "What about me?"

He pulled her to him. "Sarah darling, I did something for you this afternoon you might think rash." He took a deep breath. "I bought the millinery shop."

Her jaw dropped. "You what?!"

"That's not all." He drew closer. "I have feelings for you, Sarah. Strong ones, and if I don't act on them, I'm afraid it will be too late."

Her eyes rounded to saucers, and her knees buckled.

He caught her before she could go down. "Steady on." He held her against him to keep her upright. "Are you all right?"

She got her feet under her. "Wh-what are you talking

about?"

He stepped back and looked her over. Probably to make sure she didn't fall flat on her face. "Only this." He went down on one knee, both her hands in his. "Sarah Crawford, you'd make me the happiest man alive if you'd consent to be my bride. Will you marry me?"

Her eyes bulged as she squeaked. Could this really be happening? She shook her head, unable to believe it.

Irving got to his feet. "I'm sorry if this comes as a shock. Love strikes at the oddest times, and what is one to do?"

Her hands shook in his, and she gaped at him. "You ... love me?!" Good grief, did she have to sound so hysterical?

He smiled with a helpless shrug. "I do. Very much." He took her by the hands again. "Sarah, I love you. Marry me."

Her breathing stopped as she stared at him in shock. She didn't know what to think, what to say, and her head began to swim something awful. Everything happened at once, just before her vision blurred and everything went black.

The next thing she knew she was on the grassy ground. Irving held her and was patting her face. "Whwhat happened?"

"You fainted," he said with concern. "Are you okay?"

She stared at him a moment, her mind a blur. "What ...?"

"It's my fault I'm afraid. I think my declaration came

as a shock."

"Declaration ... oh, right ..." She smiled. "You ... love me."

"With all my heart. But you ..."

"Love you too!" She threw her arms around his neck and held on for dear life. She couldn't believe she'd blurted it out like that, but she wasn't going to take the words back. He told her he loved her and proposed! Was she dreaming? Could this really be happening?

Irving pulled her close and buried his face in her hair. "Oh, my darling, my sweet darling. I could only hope you had feelings for me."

Tears filled her eyes, and she held onto him. "I've loved you all these days past." She drew back to look at him. "I prayed the Lord would take this from me. My heart, it broke at the thought of your leaving."

He cupped her face with his hands and kissed her. A deep, wonderful, genuine kiss meant to convey his feelings. And it did. Oh, how it did.

Sarah melted into his embrace and let that kiss work its way into her heart, body and soul. She'd come so close to losing him – and she was the one pushing him away. He was too good to be true and therefore couldn't be trusted. How wrong she was.

When Irving broke the kiss, she couldn't help but cry. How could she contain her tears of joy?

"Here, now," he whispered. "There's no need for tears, my darling." He pulled a handkerchief from his pocket and wiped them away. "Please don't cry."

"Can't help it. You've ... *hic* ... made me so happy!"

Irving smiled and wiped more tears away. "I plan on making you and the children exceedingly happy." He looked into her eyes. "If you'll let me. Will you?"

She gulped. Would she? He'd professed his love for her, but was it enough? Would she still balk every time he tried to do something for her? Would her pride keep them apart? "I'll do my best." She took one of his hands and held it. "You'll help me?"

He kissed her on the nose. "Always."

She smiled, unable to contain her joy, and threw her arms around his neck again. "I love you, Irving, so much. I never thought I could love anyone like this. Yes, yes, I'll marry you!"

He held her a moment, then sighed.

She drew back. "What's wrong?"

Irving sucked in a breath this time. "You've made me very happy. But ... there's something you ought to know. It's about my brothers and me."

Her heart began to pound as the first hint of panic struck. Had he been too hasty with his proposal? She shook herself. "Wait a minute, what?"

"I know I just bought the millinery shop, but you must know, that if Sterling decides to stay here, I must return to England."

She blinked a few times. "What? Why?"

He glanced skyward. "How do I say this?" He licked his lips then looked her in the eyes. "My real name is Irving Darlington. I'm the second-born of the Viscount

Darlington of Sussex. Sterling, the firstborn, is heir to our father's title and estate when he passes. But if he decides to stay in Apple Blossom, then that falls to me."

Sarah stared at him, mouth agape. What on earth was a viscount? "Darling … ton?"

He shrugged. "We thought it best while traveling to not use our real name in order to keep our identity secret."

"I … I don't understand."

"We're not farmers, Sarah. We're landowners, yes, but of the aristocracy. We're gentlemen."

"I still don't …"

"It means we're rich." He pulled her closer. "In our case, very rich."

She listed to one side as her head swam again.

"Easy now, darling, let's not faint a second time." He held her close and kissed her cheek. "There, there. I've got you."

Sarah's eyes fluttered. "Irving … what does this mean?"

"It means, my love, that if Sterling stays, and we marry and return to England, that one day you will be a viscountess."

"I don't know what that is."

He smiled and kissed her hair. "You need not worry about it now, but can you keep this to yourself?"

"Why not let people know?" Her eyes roamed his face. How she loved this man!

"For our own safety, and now for yours. If word got

out about who and what we are, it could draw all sorts of unsavory characters this way. You don't want that, do you?"

"Do Letty and Cassie know?"

"Of course, and they've done a jolly good job of being quiet about it." He lowered his face to hers. "Can you do the same?"

Sarah looked into his eyes. "Yes."

He smiled and kissed her again. This kiss was even better than the last!

A giggle caught their attention. Irving broke the kiss, and both looked up to find Lacey, Flint, and Dora about ten yards away. Lacey ran toward them, Mrs. Whistle and Miss Parsnip's arms and legs flopping around as she did. Flint was close behind.

"Mr. Darling! Did you just kiss Mama?" Lacey smiled. "Flint!"

He came to a skidding stop and landed on his rump. "You kissed Ma?" He scrambled to his feet.

"It sure looked that way," Dora said as she caught up.

Irving sighed, got himself and Sarah to their feet, then smiled at the children. "I did. After I asked her to marry me."

Dora gasped, then smiled. "Oh, good."

Lacey stared at them with wide eyes, then tugged on Irving's leg. "Does this mean you're going to be my daddy?"

He got down on one knee before her. "If you'll have me. Yes."

Lacey tackled him, dropping her dolls in the process. "I will, I will!"

Sarah's tears started all over again as Flint slowly approached. "You'll ... be my new pa?"

Irving nodded and held out one arm. Flint looked at it a moment, smiled, then stepped into his embrace. Irving held the children close, and Sarah swore she saw a tear stream down his cheek.

Dora came alongside her. "My goodness. That's three now."

"Three?"

"Three Darlings that found love in Apple Blossom. Their parents are gonna bust a gut when they find out."

Sarah looked at her. "They haven't told them yet?"

"No, and from what I gather, when they do, there's going to be a big hullabaloo over it."

Sarah nodded, and kept her mouth shut. She wouldn't give Irving or his brothers away.

Irving got to his feet, an arm around each child, and stood before her. "Shall we tell the others?" he asked.

Sarah shook her head. "Later. First, I want to take another look at the millinery shop. Either way, I'll be selling my place."

Irving looked into her eyes, then kissed her on the cheek. "Yes. Either way." He smiled, turned, and the new little family headed back to the hotel.

THE END

About the Author

Kit Morgan has written for fun all of her life. Whether she's writing contemporary or historical romance, her whimsical stories are fun, inspirational, sweet and clean, and depict a strong sense of family and community. Raised by a homicide detective, one would think she'd write suspense, (and yes, she plans to get around to those eventually, cozy mysteries too!) but Kit likes fun and romantic westerns! Kit resides in the beautiful Pacific Northwest in a little log cabin on Clear Creek, after which her fictional town that appears in many of her books is named.

Want to get in on the fun?

Find out about new releases, cover reveals, bonus content, fun times and more! Sign up for Kit's newsletter at www.authorkitmorgan.com

Printed in Great Britain
by Amazon